Other Titles by Jill Myles

THE MERMAID'S KNIGHT

by JILL MYLES

Dedication

For Nicole Healy and Judi Sunshine. Best! Betas!
Ever!

Chapter One

Leah Sunderland stared at her body, sprawled over the hood of her car, and all she could feel was numb. It didn't feel like her body, seeing as how she stood on the curb a few feet away, though it was definitely her face spattered with blood under the mess of long brown hair.

Beside her, an elderly woman patted her on the arm. "Drunk drivers are the worst, aren't they, my dear? You were so young."

Leah pushed her thick, overlong bangs out of her eyes and just shook her head, still staring. "I don't understand. What just happened?"

The woman cocked her head, gray curls bobbing. "Well, I'm no expert on traffic, but it looks like you had the green light, and he went ahead and plowed through anyhow. He hit you on the driver's side at sixty miles per hour, and you not wearing your seatbelt...." The woman tsked at her.

"It was broken," Leah mumbled, moving around her car. "I was going to get it fixed tomorrow." It was an incredible streak of bad luck that Leah had, and the whole seatbelt thing seemed to be the icing on the cake, the latest in a long stream of things constantly going wrong in her life. "I guess it doesn't matter now, does it?" She turned away from her sprawled body and mangled car, only to find she was facing the other mangled vehicle. Sad to say, the driver appeared to be fine, if not firmly drunk. The man staggered out of his car and shouted into a cell phone, his free hand pressed to his forehead.

Tears threatened in Leah's eyes, and she blinked them away, suddenly furious. "It's not fair. Why does he get to live?"

"That's just the way things work, I'm afraid." The lady patted her on the arm soothingly. "Sometimes we walk away and sometimes we don't."

Leah eyed her new companion, something not adding up. "Who are you, anyhow? And how is it that you can see me if I'm dead?" Her eyes widened in horror. "Am I a ghost?" Her hands went to her face, feeling it with alarm. It felt like a normal face, nothing ghostly.

The woman shook her head. "No, no, dear. Don't get upset. You're not a ghost, nothing of the sort." She chuckled, holding a hand to her breast as if tickled by the thought. "A ghost, indeed. How funny." When she saw Leah's mouth quiver, she cleared her throat. "As for me, why, you can call me Muffin."

Er, okay. "If I'm dead, does that make you some sort of angel?"

Muffin blushed and shook her gray head. "Well, no. I'm actually your fairy godmother."

She did look like a fairy godmother, Leah had to admit. The woman was dressed in a bizarre ensemble of tulle and glitter, with lemon-yellow skirts and a fluffy green top. Her gray hair danced around her head in little fat sausage curls, and she had an ever-present bright smile on her lined face, even at the scene of a grisly car accident.

Plus, she could see Leah, who was dead by all accounts. So she was inclined to believe the woman, as odd as her story might be. "I have a fairy godmother?" Dumbfounded by that concept, she shook her head. "But I don't understand. I'm the unluckiest person I know." All her life, she'd had a streak of bad luck following her around. There was that time she'd gotten shot by a BB gun while walking home from school. And the time she'd caught on fire at the family cookout, not to mention a string of accidents that would make a Hollywood stuntman cringe.

Muffin had the grace to look embarrassed. "Yes, well, I didn't say I was the *best* fairy godmother, child." She cleared her throat. "To be honest, my dear, this is all my fault." She waved her hand at the two cars that resembled nothing more than kissing accordions. "I should have been paying closer attention, but I'm told these things happen to everyone." She gave a dramatic sigh.

"Well, it may happen to everyone, but it's *my* life and it's over now. I'm the one that has to pay for this."

Muffin grimaced and patted Leah on the arm again. "And I assure you, this will all be taken care of quite speedily. We'll set this to rights, don't you worry." She pursed her lips, thinking hard. "Unless you want to go to Heaven right now? Did you want to go ahead and start your afterlife?" The fairy godmother looked hopeful.

"No!" Leah protested, stung by the offer. "I want to finish living out my regular life."

"Of course, of course," Muffin agreed, her hands fluttering. "What was I thinking? It's just that it would solve all my problems if you *did* happen to want to go to Heaven now." At Leah's dark look, she smiled again. "But of course not. You're young, and you're pretty. Naturally you want to do all the things that young people like to do." She winked at Leah reassuringly. "We'll fix this. Not to worry."

Leah couldn't help *but* worry, of course. After all, it was her body sprawled on the car, and it looked rather broken. In addition to the glass that was sticking out of her forehead, her neck and back were bent at a rather odd angle that didn't seem like a fixable one. She sat

3

back down on the curbside and waited for Muffin to come up with something feasible and tried not to panic too much about what had just happened. Shock had numbed her mind; all of this seemed like it was happening to someone rather far away, not to her. The woman on the car hood was a stranger, not a young woman two days away from receiving her degree in fashion design, ready to take on the world.

Minutes ticked by, and Leah watched Muffin with expectant eyes. The fairy godmother wouldn't meet her gaze, however, and paced up and down the street that had now filled with cop cars and ambulances, and paramedics swarming over her car.

"I can't think with all this noise," Muffin muttered, reaching into her purse. She pulled out a thin, glowing wand and shook it in the air.

Time stopped around them. The paramedics froze in place, the lights on the ambulance stopped flashing, and even the wind stopped whipping Leah's long hair into her face. The world was silent.

Muffin beamed. "Isn't that much better? Now I can think." She dug around in her purse again and pulled out a small book - *Grimm's Complete Fairy Tales*. Muffin licked one finger and began flipping through the pages, her lips moving as she scanned them. "I'm sure there's something in here that will fit our situation."

"That's a book of fairy tales," Leah pointed out. "I don't think there are many car crashes in those."

The fairy godmother tsked at her again. "Ye of little faith," she chided. "While your particular scenario might not be ideal, I'm sure we can find the perfect solution in this handy little guide." She patted the book.

"But they're *fairy tales*," Leah protested, feeling that she had to restate the obvious.

"My dear," Muffin said, looking over the rims of her oversized glasses. "I am a fairy godmother. Fairy tales are my area of expertise."

Leah fell silent again, positive that any argument she made at this moment would fall on deaf ears. Instead, she looked down at her dirty white sneakers and ground a pebble underneath the sole. Would her family be upset that she was dead? She doubted it. Her father lived halfway across the country and she hadn't seen him in a decade. Her mother was long dead, and her only brother had lost contact with her years ago, right after she'd refused to let him borrow her college money. She doubted anyone would miss her at all. The thought was a sad one.

"Ah," Muffin exclaimed at last. "Here we go. An old personal favorite of mine." She hugged the book to her breast and looked excited. "Now tell me, do you like the water?"

Wary, Leah nodded. "I like the beach, if that's what you mean."

Muffin did a little dance in place. "That's perfect! Now to pick the setting."

"Setting? I'm not sure—"

"Fiddlesticks." Muffin waved a hand in Leah's face, shushing her. "I will hear no protests from you, young lady. I made this mess, and now I'm going to fix it. Tell me, do you prefer an Arabian prince, a French lieutenant, or an English baron?"

Huh? What was she talking about? "I don't care," Leah said. "I just want to know what it is that we're going to be doing."

"It's a surprise, but you'll like it. I promise. Now pick something."

"You pick it. I just want to go home." Go home, curl up in her pajamas and hope that she never met another fairy godmother... or another drunk driver, for that matter.

5

Muffin looked disappointed that Leah didn't share her enthusiasm. "My dear, you can't go home. You're dead in this time and place." When a look of panic crossed Leah's face, she hastened to add, "Which is why we'll just place you in a different time and place. Now, if you're not going to pick, I suppose I'll pick something for you." She rushed through her words with a breezy smile and took Leah by the arm. "Now close your eyes."

"But, Muffin," Leah protested. "I don't know that I want to go to another time—"

"Nonsense. It beats being dead, doesn't it? Don't worry. I've got a lovely place picked out for you. Now close your eyes and count to ten or this could get ugly." The look on her warm, grandmotherly face became stern and serious.

Disturbed, Leah closed her eyes and took a deep breath. "One Mississippi," she began, and counted all the way up to nine. The world around her was silent, the only sounds were Muffin's nervous breathing and the rustle of pages flipping.

When she hit ten, the world became silent. Her nostrils filled with water and she suddenly began to choke. Her eyes flew open and she screamed.

Chapter Two

The world around her was water. Water filled her nose and her screaming mouth, and she felt it flood into her lungs. Her hands thrashed in the cold depths and she panicked, looking for anything to hold onto in the darkness. What had happened?

A burning sensation took over her legs and they cramped and seized, pulling together despite her struggles. The burning pain flashed on her ribs as well, and she put her hands to her head, writhing in the surprising pain. Her legs stiffened, and then there was a blessed numbness. Leah curled up around herself and waited for death... again.

Nothing happened, though. Not for long, long moments. She floated in the silent brine, waiting, but all she felt was the in and out flex of her chest as she breathed.

She was breathing. *Underwater.*

Startled, she uncurled slightly and her hands flew to her abdomen. Thin slits rippled just under her breasts, and when she experimentally tried to inhale, she felt her lungs fill with water again, but it didn't hurt. She could breathe it, and it felt as natural as air. Her hands slid over the rest of her body, exploring for any new and sudden changes.

Her clothes were gone. That was the first thing she noticed as she brushed her hands over her breasts and then her bare arms. No shirt, no bra, no nothing. Her searching hands slid down to her legs and she stopped short. Something warm and scaly covered her pelvis and her thighs, and she slid her fingers down further, feeling out the situation.

Good God, she had a tail!

A panicked scream ripped from her throat, but it only came out as bubbles under the water. She tried to thrash her legs and found that they refused to part or do anything other than flip her fins – like it or not, she was stuck with a tail. Frustrated, she gave it a sharp slap against the waves and was surprised to feel it propel her forward.

Well now, that was kind of neat. She experimented with flapping her tail again, and found a good method of swimming, even if it was a bit awkward. If she thrust her entire body forward and then moved in an undulating fashion, she managed to swim at a fairly rapid pace. The taste against her lips was salty, and the water deep and cold, so she assumed it must be the ocean. But where and when?

And where was Muffin?

Instinct told her that heading 'up' in the water would lead her to the surface, and that was what she did. She realized that the waves were growing rougher and the sea around her brighter as she headed to the top. Her head surfaced a few scant moments later, straight into a rainstorm. Cold, icy rain pelted her from above, and she stared around her in surprise as the rough sea slapped her in the face.

It was nighttime, and thick clouds roiled overhead, threaded with lightning. Nothing but open sea lay in front of her, but when she turned around, she spotted a thread of shore behind her. Encouraged, she dove back underwater and began to swim in that direction, purpose in mind. She had to find Muffin and find out what was going on.

And why, of all things, had the woman turned her into a mermaid?

The shoreline came closer, and Leah could make out jagged cliffs perched atop the sandy bank. Seated on a nearby rock, Muffin sat in her fluffy yellow and green dress, her purse clutched in her lap. She looked like she was waiting on something — or someone.

The sight of her fairy godmother spurred Leah forward and she swam the distance between the two of them in record time. When the water became too low despite even that and her tail was too heavy to go forward, Leah paused on the rocks, panting. "Muffin," she called, waving a tired arm in the air frantically. "Muffin! Over here!"

The fairy godmother glanced over and waved back. "Hello, dear! Come to shore and we can have a nice talk."

Frustrated, Leah slapped the water with her hand. "I can't! You've turned me into a half-fish!"

"Not a fish," Muffin called. "A mermaid. Now come out of the water. I promise it'll be fine."

"But I have fins for legs," Leah protested again. The chill night breeze was getting to her and shivers and goose bumps covered her skin. "How can I get up to where you are if I'm trapped in the water?"

"Silly girl," Muffin chided. "Once you're on land, your legs will form again. It's not like you're stuck in the water forever. Don't you know anything about mermaids?" She primped her dry, curly hair and waited.

"Guess not." Leah muttered. Using her arms, she dragged her body across the submerged rocks and onto the pebbly shore. Once beached, she lay panting, trying to breathe gulps of air that had become too thin for her gills. "I'm... still... a... damn... fish."

Muffin smiled down at her. "Be patient, my dear. Give the magic a chance."

She lay on her back and waited for the magic to kick in. After all, she had little other choice in the matter. Her gills fluttered helplessly as she waited, chest rising and falling as she desperately tried to breathe. It wasn't working. Panic set in.

She opened her mouth to protest when a violent surge took over her lungs, and they began to burn. The next thing she knew, she was on her stomach, vomiting seawater as her body burned with unnatural heat. The pain in her legs was excruciating as she felt them separate and reform.

It was also over within a matter of moments. Her toes twitched as she took a deep, gasping breath. "Good lord. That was awful."

She felt Muffin pat her on the head. "I'm sure you'll get used to it, my dear. It's the whole exchange between water and sea – the body can't handle both at once."

"Why do I have to handle it at all? Why couldn't you have left me where I was?"

Muffin shook her head. "It's not that simple, my dear. I could have put you back into your body, but that wouldn't have worked. It's much easier to start with a clean slate."

Leah struggled to an upright position, feeling like she'd just run a marathon. Her legs trembled, and her arms shook with fatigue. "I don't understand. Why a mermaid?"

The fairy godmother shrugged. "You needed a fairy tale, so I picked for you. It could have been worse. I could have picked Bluebeard." She patted Leah's wet head and removed a damp tendril of seaweed. "All you need to do is accomplish your goal and you'll win a second chance at life."

"My goal?" Leah sputtered, trying to arrange her hair over her breasts for maximum coverage. It just barely brushed against the tips of her nipples – not nearly as concealing as she'd like. "What goal is this? Is this a contest?" Anger stirred within her. She'd rolled with the punches until now, but this was getting ridiculous.

"My dear," Muffin said, and gone was the soft, grandmotherly tone in her voice. "Just because I am your fairy godmother does not mean that I can do whatever I like. There are rules we all have to play by. You must complete your task, and when you do so, you shall have earned the right to continue on your path. No more, no less. Understand?" She leaned down and fixed a baleful, beady eye on Leah, who could only nod in surprise. "Wonderful. Are you familiar with the tale of The Little Mermaid?"

Leah wrapped her arms around her torso, shivering. The wind was biting into her bare skin, and sitting here huddled on the ground wasn't helping much. Not to mention, the shock of the entire day was finally setting in. "Th-there's a mermaid," she ventured, thinking hard. "And she falls in love with a man, and…" She stopped. "And she has to make him fall in love with her within three days or she turns back into sea foam?" Frightened, she clutched Muffin's hand. "I have three days until I turn into *sea foam*?"

"Three days?" Muffin chuckled. "Of course not, dearie. Don't be ridiculous. You have a month."

"A month?" Leah's voice ended in a near shriek. "A month to make someone fall in love with me?"

There was a shout down the beach, and Muffin stood, straightening her skirts. "Ah, here we are. Your friends shall be here soon, my dear." She disentangled herself from Leah's clinging hands. "You must make the prince – well, actually he's a baron, since princes are dreadfully difficult to come by – fall in love with you in a month's time or we'll be taking that trip to Heaven after all." She gestured to the choppy, gray waves of the sea. "Don't forget to take your dip back in the sea every day, my girl, or you'll become ill. Stay away from water and you'll maintain your human form. Understand?"

"But—"

"And most importantly – you must not let your baron learn your mermaid secret. If he figures out that you can grow a tail, you automatically lose the game. Got it?"

"Wait, no. I don't want to do this," Leah protested, clinging to Muffin even as the old woman tried to walk away. "Please, don't leave me here." She hobbled after the woman, her legs stinging with each step. "I'm all alone."

"Not all alone, my dear," Muffin said. "Royce will be with you. Just remember the voice thing." She tapped her throat and then waved goodbye. "Good luck!"

"Who goes there?" A shout came down the beach. It was a male voice and an angry one, too. "Halt!"

Muffin vanished at the sound. Leah opened her mouth to protest, but no words came out. Shocked, her hands went to her throat, and she tried to scream. Nothing but a distressed squeak escaped, and she recalled the other part of *The Little Mermaid*. The mermaid had no voice while she had legs.

Oh, freakin' *wonderful*.

Another male voice sounded behind her, and she heard the jingle of what sounded like armor and the soft neigh of a horse. "Is that a woman?" came a man's incredulous voice.

Slowly, Leah turned on one of her throbbing feet, her arms crossed over her breasts, and stared into the faces of an entire brigade of knights, mounted on their horses. They were covered in chain mail and carried shields and torches. The one in the front was twice as large as the others, and he wore no helm to mask his cold, stern face.

He scowled down at her. "Who are you, wench? Answer me."

Leah fainted dead away.

Chapter Three

Women always ruined a good, solid plan, Royce thought. He stared down at the naked one at his feet and frowned, turning to his second in command, Giles. "I thought you said that no one knew we were coming?"

"No one knows, my lord," Giles protested. "Why would they send a naked wench out here on the beach at night? In a storm?"

The man had a point. The woman *was* rather naked and alone on the sand. He'd seen her wandering from afar, and wasn't quite sure what to make of her. And when she'd seen them, she'd become frightened and fainted. That marked her as one of the enemy. Still, what to do with her now? His men waited behind him, itching for the signal to attack, and then they would be free to retake his ancestral keep, Northcliffe.

Hell. He was going to have to take her with him.

Ignoring the surge of anger that rushed through him, Royce FitzWarren dismounted from his charger and strode across the sand to stare at the prone body of the woman. He couldn't tell if she was a lady or a peasant, young or old; her body was covered in sand and gooseflesh. A long sweep of murky dark hair covered her face. He took off his long cloak and wrapped it around her, then tossed her over his shoulder. She had a surprisingly long form for a woman, but her body was light and he hoisted her over his shoulder with no effort, resting her body against the chain hauberk that covered his shoulder.

"Christophe," he called, looking for his squire.

"Here, my lord," the boy called.

When Christophe arrived at his side, Royce dumped the girl on the squire. "Take her and keep her out of the way until we've taken the castle. I'll not have a spy wandering back to warn them of what we plan tonight."

Christophe nodded. "Aye, lord. What should I do if she wakes?"

The baron was already scanning the keep nestled atop the high cliff. "Tie her up if you must. Just don't let her out of your sight."

Dubious, the squire looked at the burden in his hands. "Aye, lord."

Royce remounted his horse and drew his sword, gesturing to the castle in the distance. "No longer shall we be kept from what is ours." He grinned at his men. "Tonight we sleep in *our* keep!"

Leah awoke with a pounding headache. Something hard lay beneath her and a soft fabric that reeked of sweat had been flung over her body. She could still smell the sea, but it was not as close as before. The scent of smoke was nearby, and she could hear the soft chatter of men. Her eyes flew open at the last – she must be in the stranger's camp.

A face loomed over her suddenly, too close for comfort. A scream threatened to rise from her throat, but nothing came out when she opened her mouth other than a strangled gasp.

The face broke into a wide, gap-toothed smile and she focused in, realizing the person staring back at her was a young man. "Awake now, miss?"

She sat up slowly, one hand going to her pounding head and nodded. Her surroundings were dark and smoky – it looked like a tent of some sort. She lay half on a metal shield, her legs sprawled in the mud. A sputtering torch in one corner of the tent gave off the only light, and the rest of the shelter was filled with the scattered clutter of armor and possessions that likely belonged to one of the warriors they had passed on the way in.

"What's your name, miss?" The boy crouched beside her and offered her a cup of something to drink.

Leah reached for the cup and found it moved just out of her reach again.

"Your name," the boy pressed. "Or you'll not be getting a drink."

Frustrated, she tapped her throat, gesturing that she had no voice. She reached for the cup again, only to have it moved out of reach once more.

"I'm afraid that won't do, miss." His friendly voice had taken on a hard edge. "If you're a spy, you won't be leaving here before you share your secrets with the Lord FitzWarren. He'll get it out of you."

A spy? That was ridiculous. Leah gestured at her throat again, growing irritated with the boy's game. She tried to mime that she couldn't speak, but he ignored her, turning and replacing the cup in the bucket nearby and then taking it with him when he stood.

"You're to stay here until the master returns," the boy commanded. "If you move, I'll have no choice but to tie you up, and I don't think either of us will like that. Understand?"

Leah nodded, scowling. She hugged the sweaty length of cloth closer to her naked body. How on earth was she going to communicate with anyone if she couldn't speak to them? If they thought her a spy, she was in a big mess of trouble. Given the fact that she couldn't speak to defend herself, they'd all think she was a liar.

Damn fairy godmothers.

The tent flap flew open a short time later, and a cold breeze swept in, brushing the salty tangles of Leah's hair off her shoulders. Leah craned her neck in anticipation, trying to see who entered. If it was Muffin, she'd forgive the batty old woman for her meddling if she'd just get her out of this mess. She hugged the cloak closer to her and stared at the large figure that stood in the doorway, blocking out the light from the torches.

It wasn't Muffin. Though his face was shadowed, she knew instinctively from the sheer bulk of his form that this was the leader from before, the one who had scowled down at her from his massive horse. She clutched the cloak tighter about her and wished that she had more separating her from the strange man than just a smelly cloak.

He was handsome; she'd give him that much. His face was a study in long, chiseled lines, and his nose was a tad too large and sharp, making his features hawkish and stern. Ragged locks of black hair brushed against his shoulders, plastered against his head with sweat, and he lifted a hand to brush them aside. His eyes were dark and the set of his finely-sculpted mouth was grim.

Leah watched him as he moved inside the tent and sat down on a stool across from her, pulling off a shirt of chain-mail links. His squire rushed over to help him, and his eyes turned to her once he was free from the confines of the vest. She could see that his padded shirt underneath was soaked with sweat and a darker rust color that she hoped wasn't blood. He scratched at the sweaty clothing and gave her a lazy, bored look. "Has she talked yet?" he asked the squire.

"Nay, my lord," the squire responded, sounding quite disgusted with the fact. "She will not speak. How fares the battle for the keep?"

"Well. It goes well." The lord looked rather weary, but a hint of a smile touched his mouth. "With luck, we should be breaching the walls before tomorrow evening."

"That is good news, my lord," the squire enthused, handing him the dipper of water. The stranger drank two full dippers in front of Leah and sighed with delight afterward.

Irritated and thirsty, Leah scowled at the two of them and rather hoped they'd leave. He looked like he was a rather foul type, conquering someone else's castle. Muffin had made a huge mistake in sending her here. No way was she going to try and seduce this guy into falling in love with her just so she could have a second chance at a life.

She thought of her dead body, sprawled over the hood of her car, and remembered Muffin's words. *I can send you to Heaven right now, if you wish.* Not exactly a stellar option. Leah wanted to live, and badly. A lone tear streaked down her cheek and she brushed it away, angry that she'd cry in front of the strangers.

"God's blood, she's crying." The baron gave a weary sigh and ran a hand down his face, rubbing at the beard stubble that covered his chin. "Leave us alone, Christophe."

Leah stiffened. Warning bells rang in her mind, and she eyed the man seated before her as the squire hastily exited the small tent.

"Well now," the man rumbled, tilting his head to regard her. "Since we're alone now, do you still wish to continue with this pretense?" His voice was a low, smooth masculine bass.

She lifted her chin and gave him a haughty stare, tapping her throat once to maintain her story.

"Still holding onto that, eh? Suit yourself, if that's how you want to be. Like it or not, though, you're staying with me until I hear you speak."

Leah's eyes widened and she clutched the fabric tighter around her. She pointed at the tent and raised an eyebrow. Then she pointed at the ground, as if to question, *here*?

He seemed to understand her well enough. Scratching at the sweaty, padded shirt, he yanked it over his head. A bare, tanned chest rose in front of her, and Leah blushed, trying not to stare, which proved to be more difficult than she'd imagined. For one, he was gorgeous. A light sprinkle of dark chest hair covered his chest, narrowing down to a not-so-subtle line down his middle. The more eye-catching part of his half-nude body was the myriad of scars that covered his torso, all of them healed and all of them ugly. No easy life here.

"Do you see something you like, wench?"

Jerk. Leah's eyes snapped shut and she averted her face. How humiliating that he should catch her staring at him. She heard his low chuckle, and felt his fingertips brush underneath her jaw, forcing her head back toward him.

"Look at me," he demanded, and Leah reluctantly opened her eyes. Dark, piercing black eyes stared back down at her, and he studied her face. "Something about you is odd."

Her heart hammered in her breast and she jerked away from his fingers. What did he think was odd about her? Was she still scaly here and there? Had he already figured out that Muffin had turned her into a half-fish that he was supposed to fall in love with?

Not that she didn't have her doubts about that in the first place.

At least *she* didn't have to fall in love with him. Her heart was hammering so hard she'd likely die of a heart attack first. He didn't seem very likeable.

And he was still staring at her. "You're trembling." A hint of a crooked smile touched his lips, and Leah felt her heart thud in her breast. His features were arrogant and harsh, but when he smiled... she could see why Muffin had picked him.

Damn fairy godmothers.

Leah rubbed her arms to indicate the cold. She hoped he'd believe that she was covered in goose bumps because of the chill in the air, not because he'd flashed her a devastating grin.

"Cold?" He raised a black eyebrow at her mockingly. "You can have something warm to wear the moment you speak."

She resisted the urge to flash him the middle finger and scowled instead.

He reached over again, and Leah stiffened automatically. To her surprise, he grabbed her hand and took it in his own. Warmth shot through her cold fingers at the touch of his hand, and Leah felt a blush creep over her cheeks again. It felt rather disconcerting to have a massive knight cradling her hand as she sat in front of him, wrapped in nothing but a blanket.

His thumb stroked across her palm. "Well, you're no common girl from the village. Though I had my doubts about that to begin with." His dark eyes focused intently on her face.

Leah found herself trapped by his gaze. She glanced down at the hand in question, then back up at his face, her eyes inquiring.

The baron's thumb stroked across the soft meat of her palm again. "Too soft," he explained. "You haven't done a day's worth of hard work with these hands. These are a lady's hands." He lifted the palm of her hand, as if he would kiss it. "A lady or a whore," he amended.

Leah snatched her hand from his and curled her fingers into a fist, aiming for his nose.

He caught her hand easily, laughing at her efforts. "So, the little mute is a spitfire. I've heard Rutledge prefers his women fiery." His free hand reached out to touch a lock of the thick bangs that fell over her forehead. "Though why he would mangle your hair is beyond me. Did you displease him in some fashion?"

Confused, Leah pulled her hair from his hands and shook her head. What on earth was he talking about?

"Still refuse to talk, eh? You're a very loyal wench, then. What did he offer you to infiltrate my camp? Money? A name for your son? Jewels?" He reached out and gently stroked her cheek with the back of his hand. "Love? Surely you know that Rutledge was born with a black soul. He has no love for anyone but himself."

Her senses tingled at his soft touch, and Leah jerked away again, shaking her head over and over again. He was all wrong. He thought her some lord's whore, paid to come and infiltrate the enemy's camp? Was he crazy?

Leah looked the baron in the eye and tapped her throat with her fingers again.

Anger flared in his dark eyes, and she watched his jaw tighten. He stood, looming over her, and she instinctively backed away, the cloak clutched close to her body. "What would it take to make you talk, woman?" He was on Leah in two seconds, his hand wrapping in her hair and angling her face before his. "Would you speak if I kissed you?"

Leah's eyes were glued to his face, wide and wary. A flicker of fear shot through her—what did he intend?

"Would you speak if I tossed you on these blankets and plowed your belly? Would you give me moans of fear, or of delight?"

She tried to shake her head, and found it pinned too tightly in his hand. The only thing she could do is watch his mouth as his deadly words caressed her cheek. One hand worked free of her blanket and she shoved at his chest weakly, trying to push him away.

"You," the baron spoke again, his voice whisper soft, "can tell your Rutledge that Royce FitzWarren has no need of raping women to get what he wants. Unlike him, I am not an animal." He flung her away and stalked out of the tent.

Leah huddled in the corner of the tent, her body racked with tremors. She had thought she'd be seducing a man, not a freaking *psychopath*.

Chapter Four

The baron's war camp never slept. It was just as well; Leah couldn't sleep either. Worry and stress kept her from relaxing long enough to fall into the bliss of sleep. Tense, she remained huddled in her corner and wondered who she would see next – the surly squire Christophe, dotty fairy godmother Muffin, or the arrogant baron himself?

After endless hours of being left by herself, Leah's legs–which had been tingling up to this point—began to throb with hot flashes of pain. A quick touch to her skin showed that it was dry and feverish, and she remembered Muffin's words—she must get her legs wet nightly to keep her health.

How on earth was she going to do that stuck in a tent in the midst of a camp?

The strains of a loud, raucous song reached her isolated tent, and Leah stuck her head out the door tentatively, looking around. The sky was still dark with just a hint of pink on the horizon. Dawn would be coming soon, and her legs throbbed painfully in anticipation. There was a large central fire in the distance between the sea of small tents, and the men ringed around that, singing loudly.

It was the perfect chance to escape, were it not for the boy that stood in front of the tent door, scowling fiercely at her. "Get back inside," Christophe yelled, lunging toward her.

With a squeak of distress, Leah ducked back into the tent, breathing hard and waiting for him to follow her in and chastise her – or worse.

To her surprise, he didn't. When she heard his exclamation of disgust before the tent became silent again, it puzzled her. He didn't bother to check as to why she was trying to escape?

Her eyes focused on the back of the tent and a small hole in the thick, rough fabric and a plan formed in her mind. The edges of the tent itself were buried in the muddy earth, and she didn't know if they were bolted down on the other side. Digging through would take too long. But a hole in the fabric? A hole she could easily slip through.

She used her fingers to worry the small hole into a larger one, and then larger still, pulling at the weak edges of the fabric and edging it lower. It took maybe an hour of intense effort since she was trying to be quiet, but, by the time she was done, she had a hole big enough to shimmy through.

Leah tossed the cloak through the hole and then crawled through. After five minutes of creative wiggling, she was through and found herself on the other side of the tent, in the middle of camp. Nobody was nearby, and she gathered her cloak around her body again and headed out of the camp, ducking behind each dark tent as she stole away. Some unnatural instinct told her that the sea lay to the south of the camp, and her throbbing feet led her in that direction.

She had sand between her toes and the water lapping at her feet before the dawn was even on the horizon. The moment her legs touched the water, her feet seized up in a wave of pain, startling her and causing her to pitch forward into the tide. Her legs jerked and clenched, and waves of agony shot over her. Within moments it had passed, and her tail flicked in the water, just as her gills rose and fluttered with each deep, watery breath she took.

The sea was a welcome respite from the harsh reality that she had been tossed into. No warlords, no bitter squires, no medieval world, just her and the dark, comforting sea. She swam for hours, easing her mind. She couldn't hide in the sea forever, much as she would like to, unless she wanted to fail the task Muffin had set before her.

The thought of dying permanently was even less appealing than her other options. Leah headed for shore reluctantly, swimming in closer to the jagged rocks. The anticipation of the pain that would hit her body when she left the water was not a pleasant one.

"Yoohoo," called a voice from the shore. In the distance, the fairy godmother waved her hands excitedly.

Leah swam close, waving a hand in return. Relief poured through her. She wasn't alone anymore. Muffin could fix this.

"How are you doing, my girl?" Muffin put a hand to the overlarge pink straw hat that covered her gray curls. She was dressed in a matching pink sundress, and looked like she was heading for a day of vacation on the beach – the irony of which was not lost on Leah.

Leah pulled herself halfway onto a nearby rock to rest her tired, wobbly arms, and patted her throat, reminding the old woman of the curse.

Muffin waved her hand dismissively at Leah's gesture. "That only works for the locals, my dear. You can talk to me. Try it."

She tested her voice, and found that it worked after all. "I can talk," she called, surprised. "Why can I talk now?"

"I'm not exactly part of this setting, my dear, so you can talk to me as much as you like." Muffin beamed and slid her sandals off, wading into the ankle-high tide. "Lovely weather, isn't it? I just adore Cornwall."

"Is that where we are?" Leah eyed the rocky shore that surrounded them. "Great Britain?"

"It won't be anything but England for several centuries. This is the fourteenth century, if I recall correctly."

Leah's head spun as she tried to comprehend that. The fourteenth century? That was six—no, seven—centuries before she had even been born. "Why are we here?"

"Why, because you let me pick. I do prefer the medieval feel of things to any other time period. So romantic with the knights and their ladies fair and such. You're lucky, though. You missed the Black Plague by about a decade."

"Oh, yes, I am just *so* lucky," Leah said sarcastically. "Those men up there are trying to steal that castle from someone else. They're rude, uncouth, and they won't give me a scrap of clothing. One of them even called me wench. And last night? I had to use the bathroom in a bucket. It was *awful*. And their leader thinks I'm some sort of slutty spy!"

"Oh dear." Muffin's brow wrinkled. "That could be a bit of a problem. You've got to make him fall in love with you and you've only got twenty-nine days left. He might like the slutty part, but I'm not sure about the spy thing."

"Why do I have to make him fall in love with me?"

Muffin seemed surprised at the question. "Why, because that's how the fairy tale ends, my dear."

Leah buried her head in her arm, leaning against the thick slab of rock. "Why couldn't you just let me go back to my old life?"

"Your old life was long gone, child." There was a thread of steel in Muffin's voice. "There's no sense in lamenting over what you've lost and crying like a spoiled child. You wanted another chance, I'm giving it to you. These are the rules I have to follow as a fairy godmother. Feel free to give up at any time and let yourself drown." She stepped out of the water and put her sandals on her feet, giving Leah an offended look. "Let me know when you're ready for my help."

"I need help now!"

Muffin shook her head and winked out of existence. "I'll be back tomorrow night." Her words floated on the windy air.

Just like that, she was gone. Leah groaned and slapped the water in annoyance, and then dragged herself back onto shore and lay in the sand. She had no choice. She had to make him love her.

It didn't take long for the pain to kick in. Her body began to shudder with convulsions, and seawater erupted in her mouth. Pain overrode all of her senses, and then it was over. Exhausted, she put her head to the soft sand and slept.

Something hard prodded her side. Leah twitched in her sleep, then rolled over, not wanting to wake just yet. She was so tired, and the sand beneath her felt so good.

The hard thing nudged her side again, and Leah opened her eyes a crack to scowl at whoever was bothering her.

The warlord stared down at her, his unshaven face grim and unsmiling. "You sleep like the dead, woman."

Leah gasped and shot upright, smacking her head against his by accident. She put a hand to her forehead and winced, disoriented.

The looming man grabbed her arm and hauled her up on her feet. "How did you escape my tent? Did you trick my squire somehow?"

She gave a derisive snort at that and wrinkled her nose at him. He stank of smoke and sweat, and grime creased his face. He looked utterly exhausted as well, but she refused to feel pity for him.

"You're a terrible spy." His soft words had a hard edge of amusement to them. "I daresay that the only thing you're worse at than spying would perhaps be escaping, or clothing yourself."

Leah looked down at her body with dismay. She was naked, her legs covered in sand from the beach. Her only garment – the old cloak – was nowhere to be found.

"Rutledge has excellent taste in wenches, I must say." He forced her to turn, admiring her body.

She slapped at his hands indignantly, earning a chuckle from him. As she turned away, she spotted his men further down the beach, watching their master and waiting. Humiliation burned on her face.

"Nice flanks," the baron continued, slapping a gloved hand against her behind. Leah jumped, which earned another round of amused chuckles from the baron. "Shall I walk you back to camp naked? Methinks my men would appreciate a glimpse of your treasures as much as I have."

Leah shook her head, humiliated, horrified tears streaking down her face. She ducked her face, determined not to let him see that he was getting to her.

A loud, pitiful sniff broke the silence between them, and the baron swore. "God's bones. Not more tears."

He took his cloak off his shoulders and wrapped it around her. The red material was soft and warm, and slightly damp from his sweat. Leah gratefully wrapped it around her body and gave him a timid smile, letting him know her gratitude. He wasn't such a bad man after all, just a hard one.

"Don't thank me, wench," he growled. "I've still half a mind to hand you over to my men and see if twenty of them plowing you won't cause you to open your mouth."

Her smile turned into a scowl and she stomped her foot down on his leather-clad one. He chuckled and tucked the cloak about her body, winding the cloak tightly around her so that she could scarce move her arms. "Bundled well, now?"

She nodded uneasily.

Two seconds later, he hoisted her off the ground and tossed her over his shoulder. The air slammed out of her midsection when it impacted with his shoulder, and she nearly gagged at the sensation. Then the earth began to weave and rock as he strode across the sandy beach, her body wrapped up like some sort of overlarge burrito over his shoulder.

His large hand rested on her rump, and she could feel the warmth even through the blanket. "I suppose that I shall have to figure out what to do with you, my lovely little spy, if you insist on escaping and running through my camp naked. Your presence is disturbing my men."

Leah remained silent – what could she say to that? It wasn't as if she enjoyed being naked around all these men.

"Not to worry," the baron was speaking again, even as he strode into the middle of camp. "The defenses of the castle have fallen and we shall be sleeping in real quarters tonight. Which means that the donjon is free, as well."

She shivered at that. Was he going to lock her up? She wiggled on his shoulder, trying to express her displeasure at that thought.

In response, she got a slap on her behind. An outraged squeal escaped her. He laughed at her outrage and left his hand on her backside, a feeling that Leah found distinctly unnerving.

The walk down the rocky shore and back up the cliffs to camp seemed endless. Just when her senses were nearly rocked to sleep, the world flipped on her again and she was dumped unceremoniously on her feet. Leah struggled to keep the cloak around her body and shot an angry look at her captor.

He laughed at the expression on her face. "Perhaps next time you'll hone those fine escape skills, eh my little spy?"

Leah lifted her chin and gave him her haughtiest look.

The baron's fingers grabbed one edge of her mantle warningly. "Stay close. I don't want to have to hunt you down again."

She tried to snatch the cloak back from him, but he held the corner just out of her reach, and it was causing the rest of her covering to become dangerously loose. Worried, she slid closer to him and huddled near his arm, using him to shield her against the bitter wind. To her surprise, he put a warm arm around her shoulder and pulled her close. It seemed like a possessive move, but he was warm and a good shield against prying eyes, so she let him.

"Royce," called one of the men, and to her surprise, the baron answered. So she knew his name now, she mused. It suited him somehow.

"What is it, Guy?" He turned to the tall, lanky man heading straight for the two of them.

"You wanted a quick reconnoiter of the castle itself, my lord." The man spared her a quick, scathing glance that told Leah she hadn't made any friends while she was sleeping. "The peasants are just about rounded up and the fires put out. How is your spy?"

"Determined to share my bed tonight if she doesn't open her pretty mouth, it'd seem." Royce grinned at Guy and laughed when Leah's bare foot stomped down on his own. "She's a spitfire, if not overly intelligent."

How dare he? She tried to jerk the cloak from him again. Like hell she was going to share his bed. She'd sleep in the dungeon first. She shrugged off his heavy arm and turned away, letting him know with her stiff posture that she was not happy.

Royce ignored her feeble protests and looped his arm over her shoulders again, continuing to discuss the castle fortifications with Guy and what would need to be replaced. Leah tuned out of the conversation and stared at the castle in question behind her. It jutted into the sky, nestled like a natural extension of the rough cliffs that surrounded it. A rounded tower was closest to her view, with walls spreading outward and covering the top of the cliff. Several long slits broke up the smoothness of the tower and she imagined those functioned as windows. All in all, it was a forbidding, dangerous structure, just like the man that had worked so hard to capture it.

She wondered *how* he had managed to take down such an enormous, well-defended castle. Treachery from the inside? Siege? Since she couldn't ask, she supposed she'd never know.

Something flicked in one of the slits high on the rounded turret, drawing her attention. She glanced up. Something long, thin, and pointed extended from one window-slit as she watched, and then it shifted ever so slightly.

Uneasy, she turned to the baron, who was still deep in conversation with his man-at-arms. She tugged at the cloak again, but it did no good. He ignored her, his arm squeezing tighter around her shoulders to keep her in place. Anxious, she glanced up at the window again, and saw the thin thread move ever-so-slightly again.

It was an arrow, aiming carefully for its target.

Aimed at Royce – her one shot at a second chance.

She gave Royce a violent, sudden shove, desperate to move him out of the way of the arrow. She caught him by surprise, for he stumbled over a few feet. Guy bellowed with outrage, and she heard the sound of him drawing his sword. A loud *thwack* sang through the air.

The world bloomed into pain.

She stared down at the arrow that protruded from her cloak and felt the waves of pain rising off of her arm. She'd been shot, not him.

Uncomprehending, Leah stared up into Royce's dark, surprised eyes.

Chapter Five

The world settled into a chaotic blur after that. The courtyard erupted, men drawing their swords and screaming, knights running into the castle to seek out the shooter. She remembered Royce touching her chin briefly and giving her arm a cursory look, ripping his cloak from her. When he determined that it was lodged in her arm only, he touched her chin again and then headed for the castle, Guy close on his heels, sword drawn and his mouth drawn into a grim line.

After that, Leah lost track of what was happening. She stared down numbly at the arrow protruding from her skin, noting the smooth tip that stuck out the far side of her arm, and the hot blood that dripped down her skin. She wanted to scream with the pain of it, but her mouth wouldn't work. No sound would come out.

Kind hands wrapped her listing cloak close around her body, taking care not to touch the arrow. "Come with me," Christophe coaxed, urging Leah forward. "I'll take you to the leech."

Leah jerked at that and shook her head violently. She didn't want to see any sort of leech. It sounded frightening.

He ignored her protests and pulled her along, and Leah found that she could not disobey. She was too disoriented and the pain in her arm was an incessant throbbing.

Time swerved in and out as she was half-walked, half-dragged into the chaotic courtyard. Royce's soldiers shouted orders around her, babies cried, and people were running everywhere. One man bumped into her, and the resounding shock of pain that reverberated through her arm caused her to nearly black out.

Next to her, Christophe yelled at the soldier, and steered Leah out of the way, dragging her across the cobblestones and through the courtyard to a building in the distance.

Warm hands grabbed her bad arm, brushing against the arrow, and Leah's body racked in a shudder at the touch. Her mouth opened in another silent scream.

"She's wounded," Christophe bellowed beside her, and the hands slid away.

She faded in and out for the next several minutes, and the next thing she recalled was a gentle woman's voice speaking. "Poor thing. She's trying to be so brave. Pretty little mite. Who is she and how did she get shot?"

A thick, furry blanket was shoved under Leah's chin and the cloak was pulled away from her body. Christophe's grim voice rose again. "One of the rebels was still at the arrow slits in the west tower. She must have seen him. Strangest thing – she pushed Lord FitzWarren out of the way and took the arrow herself."

I didn't mean to. Leah's eyes remained squeezed shut, her lips tight. The pain was easier when she didn't have to focus on the strange world around her.

The woman clucked, and warm hands touched her bare arm again. "And you said that Lord FitzWarren believes her to be a spy?"

"She won't talk," Christophe stubbornly insisted. "She appeared in the midst of camp, naked, and won't say a word. The only logical explanation is that she's a spy of some sort."

"Mayhap the little mite is a mute. It happens sometimes. Did she cry out when the arrow struck her?"

"No." Christophe's voice was sullen.

"I see." The woman's voice was soft, understanding. "And when Beorn nearly knocked her aside in the courtyard?"

"Nothing."

"Mmm." The woman's voice was bland. "Perhaps she cannot speak after all. She's not much of a spy if she cannot report what she finds, is she?" Before Christophe had the chance to comment, the motherly voice grew fainter, as if she were turning away. "Stoke up the fire, lad. We'll need it nice and hot. Fetch me a blade, as well. The wound's gone clear through to the other side. After we've removed the arrow, we'll sear the wound shut."

Leah's eyes flew open at that. Sear the wound shut? Take the arrow out? The damn thing hurt so much she couldn't bear the thought of anyone touching it, much less ripping it out. She shook her head, trying to pull the covers off.

A face loomed over hers, a rounded one with bright red, flushed cheeks. It wasn't a pretty face, but it was a kind one, an elder woman with her hair pulled back in a tight coronet of braids, the brown streaked with gray. "Relax, child. You can't go anywhere until we get that arrow out of your arm. Be brave."

Leah didn't want to be brave. She wanted out. She swung her legs over the edge of the odd, lumpy bed that she was on and tried to push herself up. A wave of pain shot through her arm and she nearly collapsed. "Don't move," the woman warned again. "You'll only make it worse."

Nervous, Leah's eyes searched the small chamber. It was dark save for the fire roaring in fireplace against the far wall. The bed she lay upon smelled of old sweat and musty hay, and the walls around her were bare. There was nothing to grab hold of and use as a weapon against this woman with the kindly face who was determined to burn her. Even now the woman turned back to the fire, stirring it up hotter. A whimper died in Leah's throat.

The door swung open, and instead of Christophe with the knife, it was Royce himself. He lit up in a smile at the sight of the wide-faced servant. "Maida! It is good to see you here."

The woman smiled and gave him a cheerful embrace. "It is good to see you return, Master Royce."

"Lord Royce, now," he said, pride in his voice. "And now Lord of Northcliffe, thanks to the king. Where is Rutledge?"

Maida waved a hand. "Scuttled out of the keep last night, I hear. You know these halls are riddled with secret passages. He likely crept out once he heard you were coming."

Royce came to Leah's side, his face drawn into grim lines. She averted her face, staring down at the thick blankets as he examined the arrow protruding from her arm. "Has she said anything, Maida?"

"Not a sound from her, milord. Not even when Christophe let her get smacked about by your soldiers."

Strong fingers touched her chin, angling her face toward his. "So you were telling the truth the whole time, my little silent one? You cannot speak?" The look on his face was inscrutable.

Leah wearily tapped her throat.

He swore and raked a hand through his dark hair. "It makes no sense, Maida. None of this does. It should have taken us weeks to overtake the castle, not two nights. And now Rutledge is fled to the south, taking all his soldiers with him and abandoning his castle?" His hands grasped Leah's arm and she stiffened when he snapped off the long end of the arrow. "I thought for sure the girl was some sort of spy sent by him to catch me off guard."

Great. He had gone from accusing her to talking as if she weren't here.

He seized her upper arm in a burning grip. His dark eyes focused on her frightened ones. "This is going to hurt, girl."

That was all the warning she got before he grasped the arrowhead on the other side of her arm and yanked the remainder of the arrow straight through her flesh.

Hot agony poured through her. She could feel her mouth open in a scream, but no sound came out of her throat. Blood gushed from the wound, and Leah felt dizzy with the pain. Tears poured from her eyes and she gasped like she was drowning.

Gentle fingers stroked her cheek. "It's all right," Royce murmured. "'Twill be over soon." He brushed the tears off of her cheek. "Maida will fix your arm, never fear. She was my nursemaid when I was but a boy, and she took care of me then." A hint of a smile curved his mouth. "I have no doubt she can take care of you now."

"Oh you," Maida scolded, a girlish giggle escaping her throat. "Still a charmer after all these years." She moved forward with a damp cloth and bustled past the large man, clucking over Leah's arm. "Christophe tells me that the arrow was meant for you, milord. I'm thinking you owe her your life."

"It would seem so." At his words, Leah looked up and stared into his searching eyes. He gave her an odd, appreciative look and she blushed, remembering that he'd seen every inch of her naked. He'd even hinted that she should become his lover.

Maida's touch was as gentle as she could make it, and Leah knew she was trying. When she winced at one particularly rough motion, the woman gave her an apologetic look, and Leah returned it with a faint smile of her own. "Such a pretty child," Maida clucked. "Where is that boy with the knife?"

"Here," Christophe said, returning through the door and breathing hard. "I ran the whole way." He showed Maida the knife. "Cleanest one I could find."

Leah's eyes bugged at the sight of the large carving knife with the wicked edge.

Maida took the knife from him and stuck it in the flames, wiping her bloody hands on her apron. "Almost done," she announced cheerfully.

Long, silent moments passed. Maida returned to the side of the bed, the red-hot knife held by the carefully wrapped handle. The tip of it glowed white-hot. "Hold her arms," Maida warned the men.

Before Leah could panic, both men were holding her down to the bed, even as Maida neared with the knife. Luckily for her, she passed out the moment the smell of burning flesh hit the air.

Chapter Six

Leah awoke some time later with a dull throbbing in her arm and a massive headache. Her hand automatically went to her wounded arm, and she tore the covers off to see the damage. Thick bandages swathed her upper arm, and they looked to be clean and wrapped tight. The faintest touch caused a shockwave of pain to shoot through her arm.

The crisp bite in the air told her that the fire had died and she'd been alone in the dark for some time. Since there were no windows to the room, she didn't know what time it was.

She was also still naked, a fact that caused her more than a slight bit of consternation. Did no one clothe prisoners around here? Grabbing a blanket, she wrapped it around her body and slid out of bed, her feet touching the hard stone floor underneath. As soon as she put her full weight on her legs, a wave of tingling pain shot up her legs, reminding her that she needed to get to the shore, and soon.

On silent, painful feet, she padded over to the thick wooden door. A stream of faint light shone underneath. Her hands felt along the door jamb, looking for a doorknob, and came to a thick metal bolt. She moved it out of place and tugged on the door.

It wouldn't open. She was locked in.

It didn't register at first. She gave the door another tug, thinking that she'd underestimated the weight. When the second tug was equally useless, she began to panic. Using her good hand, she beat on the door, hoping that the ineffective sounds were heard.

I can't even call for help, she thought bitterly. She heard the shuffle of feet outside the door and the low murmur of voices. Encouraged, she pounded on the door again, her hand aching and raw.

A few moments passed, and then there was a soft knock on the other side of the door. "May I enter, child?" It was a soft masculine voice, not that of Royce or his men that she had met.

Leah hugged the blanket close to her and took a few steps back from the door, sitting on the edge of the bed and waiting. A small man came in and smiled at her. He wore long gray robes, and his hair was cut in a thickly fringed cap. "I am Father Andrew. Lord Royce has asked me to sit with you for a time."

Probably to see if he could get more answers out of her, she thought wryly.

The priest pulled a small wooden stool to her bedside and sat, smiling faintly. "Do you have a name, child?"

Leah nodded and mouthed her name to him, trying to enunciate.

It was useless. He gave her another faint smile and shook his head. "I'm sorry. I don't understand you."

Frustrated, Leah mimed holding a pen and scribbling. Maybe she could write it down for him.

He watched her motions and cocked his head to the side, trying to understand. "Your hand hurts you?"

She wished she could groan her frustration.

It must have shown on her face, for the priest gave her another look of embarrassment. "Perhaps we could narrow it down, then. Is yours a common name?"

40

Leah shrugged. What was common to him?

"Norman? Saxon? You have the look of the Irish about you." When those suggestions garnered no more response than a wrinkling of the nose, he tried again. "Something from the Bible?"

Her eyes lit up and she nodded, smiling at the priest. He thought for a moment, then hesitantly asked, "Mary?"

She shook her head, and he continued down the list of names. It took some time before he worked around to "Leah?" but when he did, she exploded with excitement, grasping his hand in her good one and nodding enthusiastically.

"Your name is Leah? How lovely." He smiled at her. "And are you a noble's daughter? Or one of the castle folk?"

She shook her head, not sure how to respond to that. Peasant or noble didn't factor in to her old life. Leah shrugged and looked away.

The priest gave up at that point, letting the questioning die down. "Well, Leah, my lord FitzWarren is at a loss at what to do with you. His men suspect you are a spy, but he thinks you are the leman of Rutledge. Since he now owns all in this castle, that would make you part of the bargain. Do you understand what I am saying?"

Her mouth thinned. She understood. The baron could do what he wished with her and the priest would not do anything to change that.

She felt his hands clasp her own. "If there is anything I can do, child, please let me know. I know that you cannot give confession because of your affliction, but the Lord hears silent prayers as well. If there is anything that you need, I shall endeavor to get it for you."

She needed to get to the ocean before her legs gave her any more pain. Leah gestured at the door, and then made a swimming motion. She even held her nose to see if that had any more success.

The priest shook his head again. "I do not understand."

Leah frowned in frustration, then touched her tangled hair and made a washing motion. When faint recognition dawned on the priest's face, she continued her enthusiastic gestures, pretending to rub her arms.

"A bath?"

She nodded enthusiastically, a happy smile breaking her face. It wouldn't be as good as a dip in the ocean, but it might hold off the worst of the pain.

"But 'tis winter outside, lady. You will die of sickness."

Despite the priest's protests, Leah held to the idea, and he eventually returned a short time later with a large wooden tub and several servants in tow. They set the tub down and began to fill it with buckets of fresh, cold water. No hot bath for her, then. It was just as well.

Father Andrew handed her a lumpish gray cake of what must be soap and a wooden, wide-toothed comb. "I've asked for clothing to be found for you, though I must get it approved by Royce first." A faint frown of disapproval creased his brow, as if he didn't care for Royce's tactics. Leah was warmed by his displeasure – it meant that she had an ally, at least, and one more reliable than Muffin. "Is there anything else I can get for you?"

Leah thought for a moment, then tried the motion for 'writing' again. When that elicited nothing more than a confused response, she sighed.

"Needlework?" He pursed his lips, then smiled. "I am certain I can find something for you to embroider."

Embroidery? Er, not exactly. Leah frowned at the priest's retreating back. The room cleared out shortly, and Leah was left alone with the tub full of water. She wasted no time in sliding the bolt on the heavy door for privacy before shucking the blanket and heading for the inviting tub. A hiss escaped her when her flesh contacted the icy water, but she slid her body in, desperate to relieve the painful throbbing in her legs.

Within minutes, the pain had receded, and her gills had returned, her lungs filling with the heavy, familiar feeling of water. Her tail stuck out over the edge of the rough tub, but the effect was still the same – the throbbing subsided to a low, dull ache in her bones. Using the harsh soap, she scrubbed her body clean of salty residue and then worked on cleaning her hair. It was a snarled, tangled mess, and the soap only made the tangles worse even as it cleaned her hair. She slid down further in the tub, tail jutting in the air as she rinsed the soap from her head.

There was a knock at the door. Fear shot through Leah and she struggled to sit upright in the tub again, water sloshing on the floor beneath her. She shoved wet, tangled hair out of her face and stared at the thick wooden door across the room. Would they go away if she didn't respond?

Her long, smooth tail gave a shiver as the knock came again, harder. "I know you're in there," the voice on the other side called, sending panic spiraling through her. It was Royce. "Unlock this door."

She couldn't respond. When she opened her mouth, water dribbled out.

"Woman," he called again, his voice barely controlled with anger. "If you do not open this door in the next moment, I am going to break it down."

Panic erupted inside her and she struggled to get out of the tub. The sides of the damn thing seemed impossibly high for her suddenly, and she lacked the upper-body strength to haul herself out of the water and over the edge.

The door on the far end of the room shook with a bang, and she heard Royce grunt with anger, then rammed the door again. He was truly going to break into her room. Had he forgotten she was a freaking mute? He couldn't see her with her tail. Panic flared through her body, making her flop in the tub, gills fluttering. If he saw that she was a mermaid, she was done for. *Finito.* Muffin would haul her right back out of this bizarre world and she'd be dead forever.

Fright fueled her into lunging out of the tub as the door crashed once more, and then the tub tipped, spilling the contents all over the floor. Thick, soapy water slopped across the floorboards and made a mess of the room. Leah forced herself out of the puddle, bracing for the pain of her transforming legs.

The red-hot agony erupted. Ribs and legs burning, she forgot all about the outside world for a moment as her body convulsed in agony. Water sprayed from her mouth and she struggled to breathe for long moments...

...And then she felt warm hands grab her under her breasts and turn her over. Callused fingers touched her cheek, brushing away her tangle of hair.

"Woman?" Royce's voice touched her ears and Leah opened her eyes to stare into his concerned ones. "Are you well? What has happened?"

She buried her face against his chest, weary and exhausted. That had been too close for her liking. Her heart still hammered with fright at how close he had been to discovering her secret.

Royce's large hand smoothed her hair away from her face and he wrapped her in a blanket, keeping her close to his chest. He was a very large man, and she felt small and dainty pressed up against him, and safe. Odd that the frightening warlord would make her feel safe, when he was the very person she should be most afraid of. But he held her close, still stroking her hair.

The sound of feet on the wet floor made Leah open her eyes again, and she looked up at the priest's disapproving face. He carried a small basket in his hands and stared at the room in obvious surprise. "Is everything well, my lord?" His eyes rested on Leah and he gave Royce a questioning, reproachful look. "Did I interrupt—"

"You didn't interrupt anything," Royce growled. "She was sick. I helped her."

The reproachful gaze focused on her. "I warned Leah that she would become ill—"

Royce's eyes focused on her, and she flinched at the sudden fury in his face. "She told you her name? She spoke?"

"She did not speak," Father Andrew replied calmly. "I suggested names until she told me which one it was."

His eyes remained on her face, searching for answers she couldn't give him. "Very well." With that, he stalked out of the room, leaving her alone in a bedroom full of water and a confused priest.

Chapter Seven

Royce must have been feeling guilty, Leah mused, because someone had brought her not one, but three dresses.

The serving-maid blushed as she handed them to Leah, patting the fabric. "They're a bit unfashionable – we found them packed away with a few of the old family's things – but it'll be warm and dry." The girl seemed young – much younger than Leah's own age of twenty-four years old. Her teeth were bad and her face was too thin, but she had very pretty blond hair that curled around her face and escaped the plain brown cap she wore over her head.

Leah took the dresses in hand and gave the girl a warm smile, touching the fabric to show her appreciation.

"My name's Ginny," the girl gushed, clasping her hands in front of her and waiting expectantly. "They tell me you can't talk. Is that true?"

Leah patted her throat in demonstration, and was rewarded with a low whistle.

"Did they cut out your tongue?"

Startled, Leah shook her head. What a morbid thought. She fingered the fabric of one of the dresses. It

46

was a thick, heavy brocade of an olive-green color that looked to be quite itchy. The dress below it seemed to be the opposite – made of a thin, cottony material that was almost see-through, it was the color of eggshells. The next was the same thick brocade, but of a rust color, with tight sleeves and a line of laces that went up the back of the dress. Perplexed, she looked to Ginny and gestured at the dress.

"Do you not know which one to wear, my lady?" The girl cocked her head and studied Leah's face. "I should think the green would be a fetching color on you. It would match your eyes, and we want you to look pretty if you're to capture Lord Royce's eye." The girl gave her a knowing look and Leah blushed.

She didn't really care what Royce thought, but she nodded her agreement and reached for the green dress, holding it up against her body.

Ginny hesitated, then picked up the flimsy gown. "Mistress, you put the sherte on underneath."

Oh. Leah blushed again. Ginny'd see her for a fraud right away. She reached for the thin dress – made from unbleached muslin, if her eye for cloth was any good – and slipped it over her head.

With Ginny's assistance she was dressed in a manner of minutes, and had a better idea of what the dress was trying to accomplish. The sleeves of the undergarment – the sherte, Ginny had called it – were tight-fitting and ended just above her wrist. Judging from the way that Ginny clucked at the length of the skirt, she was a good deal taller than the former occupant of the dress. The green over-dress fit quite well until Ginny began to lace it up and then everything fit a little too tightly for Leah's liking. Her breasts were pressed up against the fabric as a long, flat bump that she was certain was not attractive.

"Well," Ginny said, clasping her hands and keeping her expression bright. "It's warm, even if it's not decent."

Leah's lips twitched. It *was* warm, and now she was free to leave this room and explore the castle – and look for an easy way back to the beach to cure the throbbing in her legs so she could get down to romancing the baron.

The leg throbbing had already begun again with the new day. Her bath yesterday had helped some, but now it was at the point where the throbbing in her legs outmatched by far the throbbing of her wounded arm.

The servingmaid handed Leah a pair of shoes with pointy toes. While Leah struggled to get her feet into those, Ginny tugged at her hair and pulled it into a knot, clucking over Leah's 'shorn' bangs. Once Leah was groomed, Ginny gestured at the door. "Did you wish to find Lord Royce and thank him for the dress? He was quite specific that it should be brought down for you."

He must have been feeling guilty, indeed. Leah nodded and followed Ginny out of the room. She didn't much care to see Royce again, but the pretense of it would at least allow her to leave the small room for a short while.

Ginny led her out of the building and through the great hall. It was nearly empty, save for the occasional servant scurrying through and a few men that sat at one of the far tables, eating and talking amongst themselves. She noticed that they grew silent when they noticed her, and she felt a flush creep over her cheeks. What were they thinking?

The girl was silent as she led Leah down a flight of stairs, which suited Leah just fine as it was difficult to concentrate on walking on her shaky, throbbing legs – and then outside into the early morning light. The sky was overcast, but bright enough to make Leah squint as she tried to get her bearings.

The courtyard was full of activity. Across the way, she saw the one called Beorn handling one of the chargers in front of a building that was most likely a stable. The square was immense, and dirty. People milled about, all eyes focused on her. Ginny, however, didn't pause for one moment as she picked up her skirts and clomped through the mud, heading in a beeline for the far end of the courtyard and the gates. Somewhat more reluctant, Leah followed her, noting with irony that she didn't need to lift her own skirts – they were short enough already.

Ginny wiggled her fingers suggestively at the guards at the gate.

"Hold, Ginny. The baron gave us orders." One guard put his arm out, blocking Leah's progress. "She's not to leave the castle unless supervised by the lord himself."

Crestfallen, Leah nodded and looked to Ginny. Well, the girl had tried. And she supposed that Royce was right in not believing her – after all, if it were up to her, she'd be running back to the beach right now, heading for the salt water to cool her legs.

As it was, she had to force a bright smile to her face. She supposed she could go back to her rooms – assuming she'd be able to find them again.

The servingmaid must have sensed Leah's distress. With a pat to her injured arm that caused Leah to wince, Ginny took off again. "Wait here, mistress. I'll get Lord Royce's squire. He'll make his lordship come off the practice field."

Leah's bright smile faltered. It wasn't really necessary to get the lord himself... she waved her hands, trying to get Ginny's attention, but the girl had run off, leaving Leah alone with the two guards, who eyed her rather suspiciously.

She made herself busy by picking a thread off of the thick brocade and admiring the fabric. A thought occurred to her and she bent over and flipped up the edge of the skirt, checking the seams there. If it had a few extra inches she could let down, it'd be perfect.

"Leah," a voice said above her, both greeting and warning at the same time.

She jerked upright, her face flushing at being caught examining her skirts, and her hands smoothing down the waist of the dress in a nervous gesture as she stared up into Royce's sweaty face.

The man was gorgeous. She'd give him – and Muffin – that much credit. Sweaty, inky locks of hair clung to his forehead, and a smear of dirt crossed his forehead, matching the shadow of stubble on his jaw. He was shirtless, too. She ducked her head so she wouldn't have to be eye level with his broad, rippling shoulders that were tanned to perfection. Unfortunately, ducking her eyes meant that her gaze was focused on his waist, and she noticed a dark trail of hair below his navel, and several rather interesting scars.

...And a pair of hose that highlighted what could possibly be the most well-equipped groin she'd ever encountered. Surely it was the clothing that... exaggerated his attributes. Face flushing, her eyes shot back to his face again.

Cool gray eyes assessed her figure much the same as she studied him, though a smile curved his sensual mouth. She noticed his gaze rested on her flattened bosom a touch overlong, and then traveled to her hem. "You're a lanky wench. That was my mother's dress and she was a tall woman, but I can see it doesn't fit you."

Leah shrugged. He may think her tall, but she was really just average height. Most everyone she'd seen – male, that is – was about the same height as her, and she hadn't given it much thought. She glanced at Ginny, who stood at the side of Christophe, and noticed for the first time how petite the woman was. Well, she couldn't be blamed if modern women ate their Wheaties more than medieval ones. She lifted her chin in a gesture of defiance and met his gaze.

50

He laughed. "Lanky, but not without pride. I'm surprised Rutledge didn't beat it out of you."

Leah flushed bright red and tried to jerk her hand out of his. She was unsuccessful, and watched with dismay as he tucked her hand under his sweaty arm and led her back into the courtyard.

"I trust you are not in much pain this morning," he leaned over and murmured to her.

Startled at the sound of his lips so close to her ear, she jerked again, trying to pull her hand away. Did he know that her legs pained her? Had he seen more than she thought in the bath last night?

But she was still here, right? So her secret was safe?

At her lack of response, he released her hand and gently touched her elbow. "Your arm, lady. I cannot think it has healed quite so quickly as you would have me believe."

Oh.

Her *arm*.

Leah's head jerked into a relieved nod and she smiled at him. Her arm hurt less than her legs did.

Her smile seemed to stop him in his tracks, and she held her breath when he reached up to touch her mouth with his fingers. "That's the first time I've seen you smile, Leah."

Flustered, her smile faltered and disappeared. *No, stupid*, she told herself a second later. *You're supposed to seduce him! Flirt!*

She smiled again, this time a big, unnatural, toothy smile.

He gave her an odd look. He leaned back in again, his sweaty face too close to hers for comfort. "Your manners are strange, but it is easy to see why Rutledge made you his. Perhaps I shall do the same."

She scowled at him and turned away, only to have him grab her by the hand once more. Jerked back into place beside him, she glowered up at him as he gave her another sensual, arrogant grin and tucked her hand in his arm again.

"I'm afraid you're not going anywhere, Leah. As my guest—nay, my property—I will control where you go from now on. There is no place that you can go that I will not have someone watching you and reporting back to me. Do you understand?" His smile was still easy, but the teasing light had gone from his eyes, replaced by steel.

Leah's legs throbbed at the very thought.

Chapter Eight

They did not bring her a bath that night, despite her tearful entreaties to Father Andrew. He insisted that she would make herself sick, and no amount of silent pleading or mournful looks would sway the man.

He left and locked the turret door behind him.

It was dark in the room, and she was unable to sleep due to the pain in her legs that throbbed in tandem with her arm. She lit the smelly candle that they'd left her and worked on letting the seams out of the rust-colored gown. After a time, the hair on the back of her neck prickled, and she turned to look over her shoulder.

Muffin sat on the edge of the bed watching Leah work. She was dressed in a long, white fur coat with a matching puff for a hat and her hair rolled in little white curls underneath the fuzzy brim. "Hello, darling! How are you enjoying England?"

Leah knotted the thread and then bit off the remainder before placing it in her embroidery basket. "You mean other than being held prisoner in a medieval castle by a man that wants to either sleep with me or kill me – and the fact that I got shot with an arrow? Or the fact that I can't get to the ocean and now my legs feel like they're on fire? Other than all that?"

The fairy godmother looked surprised at Leah's vicious retort. "My," she said, recovering after a moment. "Someone's cranky."

She immediately felt bad for biting Muffin's head off. "I'm sorry. My legs hurt like a bitch."

Warm, wrinkled hands reached over to pat hers. "I understand, my dear. Why don't you just use the secret passage and let yourself out?"

Incredulous, Leah looked up into Muffin's twinkling blue eyes. "There's a secret passage?"

"Indeed," Muffin said. "Northcliffe is positively riddled with them, as Lord Royce well knows. I doubt he knows about the one here in the tower, or he'd not be locking you up in here, but what he doesn't know won't hurt him, right?" She gave Leah a conspiratorial wink and straightened her hat. "Did you want to go?"

"Of course," Leah breathed, setting aside the mending without a second thought. "I can't believe... it's just too incredible," she murmured as she followed Muffin toward one of the inner walls.

"More unbelievable than mermaids and fairy godmothers?" came the pert reply.

Leah smiled, shifting on her painful feet. "Good point."

As she watched, Muffin bent over and pointed. "See this stone here? Third one up from the bottom. The one with the chip in it? If you push on it, the rest of the door balance will swing forward." She demonstrated, and Leah watched in surprise as a portion of the entire stone wall seemed to swing inward, revealing a dark passageway lined with cobwebs.

"Yikes," Leah said, stepping forward. "It looks spooky."

"There are no ghosts, I assure you," Muffin said proudly, trotting in behind Leah and swinging the door shut behind them. "In fact, the only dead person in here is you." She chortled at her own joke as the door sealed behind them. The tip of Muffin's wand began to glow brightly, lighting the passageway around them with a dim, cold light. "Shall we?"

Leah's throbbing legs would not take no for an answer. "Let's."

She followed closely as the small woman led her through a dark hallway, then down another dim passage. The second seemed longer and more crudely hewn. The floor was a mixture of rock and dirt, and Muffin tsked at the roots that jutted from the floor. "Not been used in quite some time."

For Leah, each step was a new flare of agony, but at last she saw a glimmer of light up ahead. As she watched, Muffin's magic wand dimmed and went out. "Here we are," Muffin announced gaily. "Now we just need to shove aside this lovely stone that's blocking the door and we'll be out." She looked expectantly at Leah.

Leah moved to the front of the small tunnel and placed her hands on the large rock. She experimentally pushed, and grunted when the stone didn't budge. "Uh, how am I supposed to do this?"

"Oh dear," Muffin said, tapping her lip with her wand. "I suppose it's all grown over on the outside. Well, that won't do, will it?" She waved her wand at the doorway and the rock slid over a few inches, nothing more. "That should give you enough wiggle room, darling. Just watch the waistline."

Leah kept her smart comments to herself and wedged her body through. She scraped her front nearly raw in the process, but she was able to get out. A quick look around revealed that she was on the rocky shoals of the beach, at the base of the forbidding cliffs.

The beach was so close it misted her face. Relieved, Leah forgot about Muffin behind her and ran for the sand, picking up her skirts and stumbling forward. So close!

Heedless of who might be around, she stripped off the under-dress – the sherte – and tossed it down on the sands, then dashed for the water. The first moment her toes touched the water her body racked into convulsions, but she welcomed them, knowing that the pain would end soon.

It did. Before she could even swim out to sea, the pain from her legs was gone and she was free again, her spirits light. Her laughter rippled over the surface of the water with the waves, her heart carefree for a few moments at least. Eventually, she dragged herself back on the shore and lay in the sand at the edge of the tide, tail flipping casually in the water. Muffin sat nearby, folding Leah's under-dress with great care. "It's day three," Muffin said. "What have you accomplished?"

Leah propped her chin on her hands. "In regards to Royce? Not much."

The fairy godmother's lips thinned with disapproval. "You're going to waste all your time. I'm not allowed to give you a third chance, Leah Marie Sunderland. Don't mess this up."

Leah said nothing, simply running her hands through the sand and thinking hard. "This whole thing is so new to me."

Mollified by Leah's apologetic tone, Muffin gave a cheerful nod. "That's more like it, girl. Just think of this as the second chance you never had in your own life. Do all the things you wanted to do before and you couldn't! Don't let it all go to waste now that you know the expiration date, child." She leaned forward on her rock, squinting at Leah with intense eyes. "Can't you think of anything you wanted to do before you died, no matter how foolish? How selfish?"

I didn't want to die a pathetic virgin, Leah thought to herself and flushed. She'd never say *that* aloud. She'd always thought there'd be time to date seriously after college. Guess not. "I'll give it some thought."

The old woman nodded, her eyes twinkling merrily. "See that you do. I think you'll be much happier for it." She glanced up at the skies and tilted her head. "We'd better get you back soon."

"Yeah, yeah," she said, and reluctantly pulled her tail out of the water. "Time to go shake my money-maker for the king of the castle."

She was back in her room and snuggled deep in the hard bed before the sun came up. Her eyes were just drifting shut when she heard the latch at the door lift. Muffin must have come back for something. She rolled over in bed to greet her.

No words came out of her throat.

Leah sat upright in bed, staring out into the darkness. Her mouth worked silently, and fright gripped her when she realized she couldn't even scream for help. A figure loomed at the side of her bed and then bent in. Leah lifted her hand to strike – to fight back, anything – and then she recognized the angle of the jaw and the shadows of the eyes.

Royce. In her bedroom?

Surprised, she lowered her hand, though she remained wary. What did he want?

He simply stared down at her. Then, finally, he said, "I thought I heard something."

Oh. Maybe he'd heard her coming up the secret passage. She made a mental note to be quieter the next time she used it.

"No, I suppose that's foolish, eh?" He sat down at the edge of the bed and she watched him. His face seemed tense, shadowed. "Foolish to think that there might still be a traitor in the castle after all. Or to think that you might be in danger – or that you might *be* the danger." A hard, humorless chuckle escaped him. "When you spend enough years in battles, everything seems to be related to it. There is no place that is not a battlefield, even your own home."

He touched her hair thoughtfully, and a shiver of pleasure shot through Leah's body at the gentle touch. "I remember the smell of the sea from long ago, when I was a boy. I never thought I'd smell it again in my own home... and yet I find that it's you that smells of the sea more strongly than anything."

She said nothing, holding her breath.

His rough fingers experimentally stroked the edge of her jaw. "Get some rest."

As if she'd be able to sleep.

Chapter Nine

The next day, Ginny showed her a room called a 'solar,' which had charming window seats and a loom that looked to be long out of use. She had no idea how to use the loom, but the window seats were the perfect spot to work on her sewing. Leah spent the day letting the seams out of her other dress and waiting for Royce to find her again.

Eventually, there was a knock at the solar door.

Once again, her inability to speak proved to be a frustrating experience. She waited patiently until the door opened, and, to her surprise, Father Andrew walked in, a gentle smile on his face.

"Hello, my child," he said. "Do you mind if I join you for a time?"

Pleased to see him again, Leah shook her head and returned his smile. The priest's presence was a soothing one.

"Are you busy?" Father Andrew took the window seat across from her and sat down, his hands clasped on the lap of his robes. His hair was mussed and a faint sheen of sweat lay on his brow. Leah assumed he must have been outside, for he looked rather flushed.

In response to his question, she lifted her sewing and gave a wry smile of demonstration.

"Ah, mending. It is good work for women with idle hands." He beamed at her.

Leah's hands stilled at the rudeness of his words. Perhaps it wasn't an insult to mock a woman's intelligence in this time, but she was smart enough to realize condescension when she heard it. She put the sewing aside.

"If you are done with your sewing, I have some things that need patching as well." When Leah quirked an eyebrow at him, he had the grace to flush. "It's for a man in the village. He—his wife died a short time ago and he's got several small children, and no family to help him."

Leah immediately felt like a heel. Of course Father Andrew had the highest of intentions. And she, suspicious woman that she was, had dared to question him. Ashamed at her own response, Leah nodded.

He seemed very relieved. "That is wonderful. I shall have him bring the clothing tomorrow and I'll drop it here in the solar, if that's all right." At her assent, he leaned forward again. "My dear, if I may be so forward as to offer my advice..."

Perplexed by his shift in manner, Leah wrinkled her brow and studied him, her face openly questioning. What was wrong?

"I'm concerned about your... relationship with the lord of the castle."

Oh? Leah quirked an eyebrow.

His features had a fatherly cast to them as he looked out the window, uncomfortable with the confrontational topic. "The rumor is that you were the leman to the prior lord of the castle. That Lord Royce found you in a... compromising situation when they took the castle."

Leah shrugged. She was starting to get a pretty good grasp of what a 'leman' was and it didn't sound too great.

"But my dear, I was here and served the old master faithfully. And I can safely say that I have never laid eyes upon you before Lord FitzWarren claimed the castle."

She froze in place. What should she say? What was a plausible excuse for showing up naked on the beach?

"I wonder… I wonder if your intentions are honorable toward Lord Royce or if they have a sympathetic slant toward Lord Rutledge."

Leah blinked at him, unable to come up with a gesture that would articulate her answer.

He patted her on the hand. "You don't have to answer me today, child. Remember, I am a priest. Anything you confess to me is sacred."

She tapped her lips with her fingertips, reminding him that she couldn't speak.

"Ah, yes." His brow furrowed. "I had forgotten. Can—
"

"What are you doing here, priest?"

Both of them turned to stare at Royce, who dominated the doorway of the small solar door. Leah slid her hands out of Father Andrew's and stepped to the side, eyeing Royce warily.

Father Andrew remained calm and unruffled. "I was speaking to the girl. She has graciously offered to do some mending for some of the townsfolk in need."

Royce's scowl did not lighten in the slightest. "She can't exactly refuse you, can she? She can't speak." A servant scurried in behind him and left a small basket by the door, then scurried out just as fast. Royce didn't twitch a muscle, simply stood, staring down the priest as if he were a viper.

"Of course," the priest murmured. "Forgive me. If I have imposed—"

Leah cleared her throat and shook her head, trying to hide the smile on her lips. How odd that Royce should try and protect her, from a priest of all things. It bordered on absurd.

Absurd, but sweet. Totally gave her the warm fuzzies.

Father Andrew exited rather quickly, the door slamming behind him. Royce remained in place, his body still stiff and questioning, and his eyes turned to Leah.

"I heard you were hiding up here, lady. I thought to bring you dinner, if it's privacy you wish." He gestured at the basket and turned to the solar door, closing the latch behind him.

She studied him as he dragged a small table from the corner of the room and produced two small stools. He was dressed in dark colors today – a dark blue tunic with a yoke collar edged in plain blue, and darker leggings. She liked the color choice on him – it made his icy-gray eyes almost blue, and they seemed warm when they looked at her. His hair was slightly damp as well, which told her that he had just bathed before coming to visit her. She had seen him in the yard earlier, training his men, and had noticed the hard work they were putting in.

The fact that he'd cleaned up and bathed just to visit her... it made her smile. It was sweet that he'd care what she thought, even if she was just an uninvited guest.

"I thought you should eat, even if you're not feeling well enough to be seen about the rest of the castle." He eyed her as he pulled the basket over and placed it atop the small table. "How is your wound?"

Leah sat on the offered stool and gave him a thumbs-up. She forgot the wound was there half the time. It still ached, to be certain, but it was a less aggressive sort of pain than her legs, and she tended to forget it.

He took her raised thumb in his hands, examined it, then gave her an odd look. "Does this pain you?"

Whoops. She pulled her hand from his and shook her head.

"Your wound. Any fever? Redness?"

She shook her head again.

He chuckled again, which only caused her ire to heighten. "You're an odd one." At her scowl, he just grinned and began to pull items out of the basket. A thick wedge of cheese, some cold meats, something she didn't recognize. Two bowl-shaped pieces of bread, one of which he handed to her. "I wonder how a girl like you became so... arrogant. Most women are meek and silent. You cannot talk, but the air is filled with your opinion and there is no doubt what you are thinking." He studied her face again, then added, "Perhaps it's that expressive mouth of yours."

The man was trying to make her blush. Leah looked away, flustered.

"Eat." Royce sat down across from her and broke off a good portion of the cheese and placed it inside his flat bread-thing, and did the same for some of the meat.

Oh. It was a plate.

He pulled something else out of the basket – two goblets and a big floppy thing that looked like some sort of odd canteen. "I apologize for the fare, but if you will not come to the food, I can only bring you what will easily carry." He placed a goblet in front of her and began to fill it with a dark liquid that smelled like wine.

Leah filled her own plate as he poured. The meat was unfamiliar to her, but she was so hungry that it didn't matter. She stacked some in her plate and took an egg as well, pausing only for a moment at the small size and brown color of it. *Food here hasn't been processed to death*, she reminded herself, *or shot up with growth hormone. It's going to look a little different.* The cheese was white and creamy, though. Her throat was dry and she reached for the goblet and took a hesitant sip of wine.

It was awful. The taste of it burned the inside of her mouth and she barely managed to swallow before beginning to cough. At his concerned look, she put the

wine goblet down and waved her hands at him,
dismissing his fears, and tried to regain her breath.

Good god, but that stuff was rancid. She made a
mental note to hint that she preferred water.

Royce began to eat as he watched her, studying her
movements. She wanted to laugh, because she wanted
nothing more than to study his motions as well, but
instead she mimicked him and picked up a piece of
cheese, nibbling daintily at the edges and trying to seem
ladylike. It was delicious, the flavor unlike any cheese
she'd tasted before – thick and rich and tangy.

After a few moments of silent eating, Royce tilted his
head and reached for his wine goblet. "You're a mystery,
Leah. One I intend to figure out."

She arched a brow at him. That sounded like a
challenge.

He raised his glass and saluted her, grinning. "You
don't believe me? Think I won't follow through?" Royce
took a lazy bite of food. "I'm a man who gets what he
wants..." His gaze roamed over her figure in the tight
dress. "Regardless of what it might be."

That certainly wasn't a surprise. She sipped at her
wine and found it wasn't nearly as bad on the second
round. She sipped more of it and gestured at the walls
around them, a sardonic half-smile on her face. It was
obvious the man got what he wanted – they were living
in a keep he had conquered only days ago.

He seemed to be able to follow her train of thought
and grinned when she gestured at the castle itself.
"Indeed. This is not the first time – nor the last – I will
see something and conquer it." His eyes grew dark, and
she flushed at his double entendre.

He was very... blatant in his plans for her. Rather
than frightening her, though, they filled her with a
nervous sort of excitement and tension. Like he was

stalking his prey... chasing her. And she wanted to be chased.

She felt heated at the thought. What had Muffin said to her? Live life as you always wanted to? Take this second chance to do everything you wanted and more? She didn't want to die a virgin. She wanted to experience love – or at least lust. And this powerful, sexy man wanted her. The feeling was a heady one, and she gave him a faint smile over the rim of her goblet.

"Do you know the story of this castle, Leah?" He changed tactics on her, staring at the walls around them, his eyes serious and expression grave. "Did you grow up here?" He glanced back at her.

She remembered Father Andrew's words and shook her head. It seemed a safe enough answer.

He nodded agreement, and she let out a tiny breath of relief.

"Do you know of the FitzWarren name?" He casually brought his goblet to his lips and drank again, his eyes avoiding her.

She sensed tension in the air, and was more hesitant with her response this time. Again, she shook her head no.

"It is the name of a bastard." His fingers gripped the goblet tightly; she could see white around his knuckles. At first, she didn't grasp his immediate meaning. His father was a creep? Then she realized – it was his parentage.

He was a bastard. Not a jerk, but illegitimate.

It seemed to bother him quite a bit, too, judging from the clench of his jaw. When she didn't automatically leap up in disgust, he turned to her, studying her expression. "It doesn't bother you that the man sitting across from you is of less than noble birth?"

Leah shrugged idly. Why should it matter who his parents were?

He seemed to take a moment to digest this, then continued. "My father and his legal wife had a rather unhappy marriage. I remember she used to slap me whenever I walked past her. My mother had been one of her chambermaids. My father did not want to claim me as his heir, but when ten years passed and he had no children by his wife, he legitimized me and named me heir to Northcliffe."

He paused, thinking hard. "It was shortly before I was to be sent away to squire when Baron Rutledge took over our castle. It seemed that my father had insulted him at a nearby tourney in front of the king, and Baron Rutledge decided to get his revenge by taking Northcliffe, which was rich with goods at the time."

Another pause and he studied her before he took another drink of wine. "I don't recall much about that night, but I do remember seeing Rutledge standing over my father. I remember my father begging for mercy and Rutledge laughing in his face. I remember that he took a very long time to kill my father."

A sick feeling grew in Leah's stomach.

"I can still hear the screams as Rutledge systematically went through the castle and began to slaughter all that did not bow a knee to him immediately. He slaughtered my father's wife. My mother." The grim line of his lips tightened. "I escaped with my younger sister. We knew of a secret passageway and hid there. We escaped to the village the next day. Baron Rutledge found us there." Very calmly, he placed his wine goblet down and gestured at her food. "You are not eating, Leah." His eyes were intent on her own.

She raised a hand weakly and shook her head. She couldn't eat while listening to his tale, as if it were nothing.

"Rutledge found my sister. We had both hidden from him – I with the blacksmith and she with the herbalist.

She ran out, screaming, when he set the herbalist's hut on fire and they ran her through."

Leah put a hand to her mouth, shaking her head.

"I hid in that stack of hay for two days, until the blacksmith forced me to come out. He fed me and sent me on my way with instructions to go to one of my father's friends, the man I was to squire with. Lord Bowland kept me hidden until I was of an age to seek out my own revenge."

The anger and strength was back in his voice, and he ignored her, turning his face toward the window and staring out it without seeing anything. "It was a long time before I became a knight. Longer still until I made my fortune on the tourney circuit, but I did. I trained my men to be the best fighters I could make them. I am now invaluable to King Henry as a vassal. Baron Rutledge could not touch me now if he wanted to." He turned back to her, his eyes steely. "But I found that was not enough for me. I wanted to break Baron Rutledge. Make him suffer as my family suffered. And I decided long ago that I'd steal everything of value that belonged to him. His good name." He smiled, and the expression did not reach his eyes. "His castle. His wealth." He leaned over and took Leah's hand in his own, bending low to kiss her knuckles. "His woman."

Before she could protest, he stood, gesturing at the table. "I will send a servant to come and clean this up after you are done. No more hiding, Leah. I intend to make it known that you are my leman tomorrow." He swept his gaze over her – a chilling, possessive look – then stalked out of the room.

Leah was frozen, a slice of cheese dangling from her fingers as her mouth gaped. He'd decided with all the force of his personality what he wanted – and he wanted her.

The thought excited her and frightened her all at once.

Chapter Ten

The next day was a long one. Not because of pain – she'd managed to sneak out to the shore late last night and enjoy a long soak in the waters. She'd stayed out most of the night and, as a result, managed to luckily sleep for most of the day.

Ginny arrived with a bundle in her hands and a timid expression on her face. "Mistress," she said, hesitant. "I know how hard you've worked on letting out your gowns..." She paused, and a nervous giggle escaped her when Leah held out the laces. "Nay, mistress. My lord Royce has given me orders that you're to wear this one. He had one of the castle women cut it down to size for you."

A vague feeling of dread crept over her and she approached Ginny, extending her hand for the new dress. She saw that it was crafted differently than the other ones. Instead of one set of laces up the back, there were two, one up each side. Soft fabric of a deep, velvety green swirled down the skirts, and Leah suspected that this one would be tailored for her tall form.

Royce wanted to show off his prize.

A bitterly wry smile curved her mouth at the sight of the lovely dress. What would Royce say if he discovered that she wasn't this Rutledge person's whore? Would he be half as fascinated with her? She doubted it.

That dark thought turned over and over in her mind as she took off her old, faded dress and allowed Ginny to lace her into the new one. It fit well, Leah had to grudgingly admit as the sleeves settled over her arms. She'd wondered about the extra set of laces when she'd first seen the dress, but now it was obvious. The different cut of the new dress allowed it to hug her curves – to emphasize her long, lean body, unlike the other shapeless gowns.

It didn't help matters when Ginny brought out a length of golden cord and settled it low around her hips, yoking the seductive 'Y' at the juncture of her thighs. *Well*, thought Leah with a hint of amusement. *That fashion concept certainly didn't leave much to the imagination.*

"You look lovely, mistress," Ginny breathed. "Lord Royce will find it impossible not to fall in love with you tonight." She brought out a comb and began to work at Leah's long hair, fretting over the bangs. Eventually she settled on a half-coronet of braids and wove a bit of golden ribbon in. "'Tis a shame that Lord Royce didn't think of a wimple for you, Lady Leah. You would look so lovely with one, and you've got a face that it would show off well."

Images of some ghastly medieval contraption perched on her head made Leah giggle at the thought.

Ginny laughed, too and tucked the last bit of ribbon into the braid. "I believe that's the first time I've heard you laugh. You should do it more often. It takes that sad look out of your eyes and makes you so pretty."

Uncomfortable, Leah gave her another faint smile and looked away, picking at a thread on one of her cuffs. Did she look sad? Perhaps that was why Royce had taken such an interest in her – he imagined her as the sad, lonely ex-mistress of his greatest enemy. Easy pickings.

She didn't want him to think of her as sad. She wanted him to fall in love with her, damn it. Four days down, twenty-seven to go.

When she finished dressing, she followed Ginny down the winding corridors to the great hall. Leah could hear the low rumble of talking voices as they drew closer. Her heart hammered in her throat, and she began to hope fervently that no one would notice their arrival. Ginny gave her an encouraging smile over her shoulder moments before throwing open the double doors that led to the main hall.

The room was enormously noisy. Crowded, too. The long rows of tables were packed full of men. Soldiers, judging by the common cut of their clothing. A few of them had knowing looks on their faces as they glanced at her, then at the head table.

Leah's gaze followed theirs. Royce sat at the front of the room, a predatory half-smile on his face that made her knees weak. His gaze shifted over her figure, outlined in the dark green dress, and then back to her face. He looked handsome tonight, she noticed, with his hair neatly combed, his face clean-shaven, and a dark tunic covering his broad shoulders. He sat at the head of his table in a massive chair with a wooden back that rose up behind him. One of his men sat to his left, and no one sat to his right.

She suspected that place was being held for her. As she watched, Royce arched a brow, taunting her. Challenging her. Daring her to turn tail and run from his staring men and the acknowledgement that she would be his leman.

She didn't. Straightening her shoulders, Leah smoothed her skirt with nervous hands and fixed a brilliant smile on her face. Let him take that. She'd be as beautiful and charming as he wanted her to be tonight.

And elusive, she decided, spotting an empty seat at the end of a nearby table. The rough-looking men gave her surprised looks when she sat down. Well, she'd eat fast and then return to her own chambers.

"Mistress!" Ginny's voice materialized behind her shoulder and she turned. "You can't sit there!" The girl sounded scandalized. "'Tis below the salt!"

Below the salt? What was she talking about? Leah glanced down the table and noticed that all the men were staring at her with rather surprised looks on their faces, and she flushed. She'd done it again – some medieval faux pas she wasn't even aware of. Quickly she stood, gathering her skirts and giving Ginny a helpless look.

Ginny took charge. She gave a firm tug and pulled Leah toward the front of the room. The look on Royce's face was inscrutable as Ginny dragged her forward and sat her in the chair to the right of his.

Leah sat, her mind racing even as she kept the serene smile on her face. She felt like she was on display at the front of the room. She glanced down at the table. There were no utensils for her, no goblet, but all the same she felt as if it had been waiting for her.

Royce had been waiting for her.

Leah clasped her hands in her lap and turned her serene smile to him.

He was not smiling back at her. A dark look shadowed his face and her smile momentarily faltered at his expression. Royce leaned in and loomed over her face, his eyes searching hers. "No matter how Lord Rutledge may have treated you, madam, when you belong to me, you do not sit below the salt. To do so is an insult to my name as well as yours. Do you understand me?"

Leah flushed. He had misunderstood her error, thinking that Lord Rutledge had sat her in a place of indignity to insult her? She was painting the man to be quite the devil, wasn't she?

When he reached for her hand and pulled it into his own, her eyes flew to his face. Gone was the grim expression, and in its place was the teasing, seductive smile he'd worn before. He brought her palm up to his lips and placed a soft kiss against the flesh. "I am glad to see you tonight, Leah. Your beauty outshines all others."

A warm flush shot through her body so swiftly she didn't have time to react. Dazed at the gentle touch, a soft sigh escaped her.

He regarded her for a moment, then gestured a servant over, motioning to his goblet. "Bring some spiced wine."

The servant nodded and returned a few moments later, filling the goblet with a hot liquid. As she watched, he wiped his mouth, drank, and then offered the goblet to her.

Was she supposed to drink after him, or was this another form of branding her as his own? Wary, Leah glanced around the room, and a quick look showed that most of the diners shared a goblet. Ah. She graciously took the cup from his hands, wiped her mouth in his fashion, remembered to beam him a winning smile, and sipped.

Hot, spicy and not nearly as overpoweringly strong as the last wine. It was delicious. As she sipped, she watched his manners as they brought the food out. Royce's hands, she noticed, were elegant despite their large size. One of the servants approached with a delicate basin filled with water and held it as Royce washed his hands. The boy turned to her and she placed the goblet aside, mimicking his actions and washing her own hands. Once done, a silver platter with a long, flat length of bread was set before the two of them. Royce took it in hand and broke it in half, handing her one portion. Another hovering servant came and served her several large chunks of dark, cooked meat that she couldn't identify, along with a few swimmy-looking green things that might have been vegetables. It looked thoroughly unappetizing.

He laughed at the expression on her face. "Not fond of eel, lady?"

Eel? As in the sea creature? Her eyes widened and she stared down at her plate. 'Not fond' was a gross understatement. She gave a slight shake of her head. Bile crept up the back of her throat, and she reached for the goblet again.

Royce leaned in again as she drank. "I cannot stand it myself, but I did not wish to hurt the cook's feelings. I've been told she's rather sensitive on such issues." He took the goblet from her hand and drank after her, his eyes on her face. "I suspect we might have to sneak another repast in the solar after this, if you're interested. Just the two of us."

Leah gave him a prim shake of her head.

He laughed, grinning at her expression. "You play the game well, lady, but make no mistake. I will catch you, and the prize shall be sweet."

A thrill shot through her at his words. Oh, she had no doubt he'd catch her – he had to if this fairy godmother thing was to be successful at all – but she intended to make him work for it.

She took the goblet from his hands this time, placed her mouth on the same place his had been, and drank deeply, watching him the whole time. Her head buzzed as the thick alcohol ran through her system, but the look in his eyes made her even dizzier.

"My lord," a page said behind him.

Royce ignored him, focusing on Leah. She held the nearly empty goblet between them like a shield until he plucked it from her fingers and leaned closer. "Keep doing that, lady, and you'll find yourself in my bed tonight." His voice was husky as he reached over and rubbed his thumb against her wet lower lip.

Feeling brave – and a bit tipsy – Leah shivered at the feeling of power his attentions gave her. She felt beautiful, eminently desirable – like the most gorgeous woman in the room. Heck, in the world. His thumb caressed her lip, doing marvelous things to her nerves, and she opened her mouth a little and bit the tip of it suggestively.

"My lord," the page said again, plaintively. "We have visitors." His voice broke. "From court."

Silence descended on the room.

To Leah's surprise, Royce shot away from her as if he'd been stung, his head whipping around. His eyes seemed fixed on something at the far end of the room, and Leah's gaze followed his.

A woman stood at the far end of the great hall, dressed in vivid red, her pale golden hair pulled back into an elaborate braided coronet. She was beautiful, with a sweet face and a dainty figure. A thick golden necklace dominated her throat, and the suggestive belt at her hips was not gold cord, but golden links.

Leah immediately felt underdressed.

"Lord Royce," the woman said, her voice sweet and shrill all at once. "Will you not come and greet your bride?"

His bride?

Royce was married?

She looked up at him in shock, hurt spiraling through her. Just when she'd relaxed her guard with the man...

He wasn't looking at her anymore. Instead, his entire body radiated tension as he stood and crossed the room to the delicate beauty. "Lady Matilda. I had no idea that you were to be coming out to Northcliffe so soon."

His voice was just as stiff as his posture, Leah noted. Gone was the teasing affection and smoldering sensuality. In its place was the curt, efficient warlord.

"I insisted on seeing *our* castle once I'd heard you were successful in retaking it." Matilda's voice was imperious as she placed her hand in his outstretched one and picked up her skirts with an elegant, pale hand. "I had no idea that it would be quite so grand... or that you had set up your whore in my place of honor."

Leah's face burned. She stood, shoving her chair out abruptly and stepping away from the table. Escape was the only thought on her mind – escape from the staring eyes, the judgmental looks of the beautiful woman, and escape from her own heartache.

A hand stopped her, grabbed her arm. She looked down and saw a red sleeve, embroidered with golden thread. Silk, her brain noted. Leah looked up and stared into the face of Lady Matilda. The woman's pretty features were twisted into a scowl. "How dare you," she hissed. "Who do you think you are, to take my place?" When Leah remained silent, the woman's grip on her arm became painful. "Answer me!"

Leah stared at her mutely and shook her head. As she watched, the woman's hand reached back, ready to strike.

The hand was stopped mid-swing by Royce himself. He clenched Lady Matilda's hand in his own, and gave her a tight smile. "That is not your right, my lady."

Immediately, Matilda's voice changed to a soft whine. "I am terribly sorry, my lord. I was just upset by the sight of her." Fat tears rolled out of her blue eyes, and she turned and buried her face against his tunic, sobbing prettily.

Stunned, Leah could only watch as Royce hesitantly patted the woman on the back. What was happening? Why hadn't he mentioned that he was engaged to this horrible witch of a woman? Tears welled up in her eyes and she fled the room, humiliated.

Her skirts tangled about her legs as she ran, hampering her progress. The castle inhabitants ignored her as she dashed through the halls, heading back to her room. It was when she turned down the wrong hallway for the third time that Leah realized she'd become lost in the maze of castle hallways and sank against one of the stone walls, tears sliding down her cheeks.

'Hurt' wasn't the best word to use. Oh no. It went so much deeper than that. Humiliated. Disappointed. Pissed. Out-and-out furious at Royce for leading her on. He'd teased her, caressed her lip, whispered sweet nothings in her ear, and she'd sat there and giggled like a fool. Leah closed her eyes, miserable.

"Leah," Royce said softly against her ear, his hands sliding over her shoulders.

Startled, Leah jerked away. The last thing she wanted was to be touched by a jerk like him. Her anger found an outlet when she smacked her hands against his chest, over and over again.

Clasping her hands in his, he pulled her close to him. "I'm sorry, Leah. I had no idea that she was coming tonight."

Not 'I'm sorry I didn't tell you'. She stiffened against him and tried to jerk away.

"Matilda de Beaumanoir is not my betrothed," he explained, looking down into her furious face. "Her father wants to merge his lands with mine, and she has great wealth. No contracts have been signed. I haven't yet decided if we will marry."

Gee, how *kind* of him. Leah tried to pull away. He wouldn't let her. His hard, massive frame held her own slender one against his, one hand stroking her hair to soothe her. "It doesn't change anything, Leah," he said, and she could hear his voice rumble in his chest. "You're still mine. I won't allow Matilda to hurt you, but make no mistake – I will have you. A wife and a mistress are two different things entirely."

She pulled back to hit him in the face with her fist, fury and anger taking hold of common sense. He grabbed her hand, and she stared up at him, all her emotions swimming in her eyes. Damn him for being attractive to her.

His mouth descended on hers and they kissed.

It wasn't a soft kiss or a tender kiss. It was a conquering kiss that made Leah's toes curl in her pointed shoes and made her blatantly aware that she belonged to him. His mouth pressed against hers, his lips insistent, and she felt his tongue slide along the seam of her surprised mouth.

Frozen for a moment, she hesitated, then opened her mouth and his tongue touched her own. She nearly lost control of her knees then, and leaned into him. He was devouring her with his mouth, and the world didn't exist outside his touch and kiss. Her nostrils filled with the scent of him – thick and masculine, and he tasted like the spiced wine she'd been drinking.

He tasted wonderful, and Leah melted against him, giving in to the kiss.

He must have sensed her acquiescence, because he groaned into her mouth, and then his hands pulled her toward him, hips against his own. "Say you'll come to me tonight."

It was like a splash of cold water against her face.

Leah jerked away from him, tearing her lips away from his wonderful kiss. How dare he try and placate her with kisses? As if it would make Matilda go away?

She shook her head at him and pushed him away. He let her go this time, which surprised and disappointed Leah all at once. She turned and ran.

Muffin was not at the beach that evening.

Leah swam just enough to ease the ache in her legs, then dressed in her shift. She sat alone on a nearby rock, watching the waves crash against the pebbly shoreline. Her mind was awash with thoughts of Royce. His kiss, the way he'd held her against him. Her lips could almost taste the memory of his.

But she couldn't forget that the hateful Matilda had called her a whore in front of everyone. Matilda, with the pretty face and beautiful gowns and who had everything Leah wanted.

Like a life.

Like Royce.

Her cheeks flushed at the thought. Did she really want Royce, or was she just falling prey to Muffin's schemes? Sometimes she wondered, but then she'd think back to the tender way he held her, or the way he kissed the inside of her palm. His thick, callused hands were always careful with her, and his eyes held a special look for her alone.

Leah sighed. Like it or not, she couldn't claim it was all entirely Muffin's doing anymore.

Which was why the betrayal stung so much. Tears pricked at her eyes again, and she dashed them away, angry at herself for moping and crying. It never solved anything, and she didn't have the time to waste feeling sorry for herself. She tilted her head and stared up at the cliffs where Northcliffe castle rested high atop the crags.

A shadow moved between the rocks.

Leah froze and turned that direction, squinting and trying to make out the small movement. What was it? A wild animal? A spy? Royce? If he caught her out here on the beach...

Cautiously, she tossed her loose kirtle over her shift and pushed her wet hair off of her face, heading slowly for the rocks to investigate. She was barefoot, and her hands clasped her skirts high above her ankles, just in case she needed to run.

"Yoo hoo, Leah!" A cheerful, familiar voice called from just down the opposite side of the beach. "How are you, my dear? What's with the long face?"

Leah turned away, glancing over at Muffin with a puzzled frown. "I... I thought I heard something." She touched a hand to her throat, realizing she could speak. "I suppose it was nothing."

Muffin patted Leah's arm absentmindedly. "Of course it is, dear. Nobody wanders around on the beach at night except me and you." The woman was dressed in a bright pink fluffy bathrobe and slippers.

"And men about to storm a castle," Leah added dryly.

The fairy godmother tittered at Leah's joke. "True indeed! How are you, my dear? How is everything going?"

Leah's jaw clenched at the question. "Did you know the bastard was engaged?"

Muffin blinked up at her. "I thought the contracts weren't signed?"

Was everyone on a different page than her? Leah frowned down at the diminutive woman. "It doesn't matter if they're signed or not – that horrible woman is here and she's... she's messing up everything!"

"Everything? Everything like what?"

Everything like Royce kissing her, she wanted to blurt out. Everything in her fragile new life that she was starting to become accustomed to.

"I see," Muffin said. "So you're just going to give up now?"

Her brows drew together as she stared down at the fairy godmother. "Of course not. I'm going to have to win him away from that bitch."

80

Muffin cackled, a loud, delighted laugh of glee. "That's the spirit, my girl! I knew there was a spitfire behind those big green eyes of yours. All it took was a little waking up." Gleefully, she rubbed her hands together and sat down on a nearby rock. "So what's the plan?"

"I haven't thought that far ahead," Leah confessed. "If she's going to be around all the time... I don't know what to do."

"You make her look bad," Muffin said. "You smile and you act pretty and you bat your eyes at him." She demonstrated, flittering long, fake eyelashes at Leah. "And when he's panting at your skirts, she'll look like an even bigger shrew."

Leah mulled it over in her head. It did sound rather simple. "But I can't talk to him... how do I get his attention?"

"You really have to ask that?" Muffin hitched up her robe and fluffed her bosom. "You're a woman, aren't you?"

A woman that wanted to die of embarrassment at being taught seduction by an eighty-year-old fairy godmother, but a woman nevertheless. "Uh, I don't think that gives me a leg up on her. Last time I checked, she was a woman too."

Muffin toyed with one of her springy curls and fluttered her eyelashes. "I think you know what I mean."

This was getting weird. "I'll give it my best."

Chapter Eleven

The next morning, she set her plan in motion.

Shortly after Leah woke, Ginny arrived with a tray for breakfast and a grim look on her face. "I'm glad you're up, mistress." She glanced at the door behind her and frowned. "A certain lady instructed that I should not bring you a tray, but force you to go and dine in the kitchen with the rest of the... staff." The girl's voice strangled on the last word. "I couldn't do that though, mistress. It's just too cruel, and you've been so nice to me."

That was loyal of Ginny, and Leah's heart warmed.

"Besides, he doesn't look at her the same way he looks at you. Like he wants to take you into dark corners and kiss you." Ginny whispered the scandalous words. "It's the talk of the keep, the way he eyes you."

Talk like that made Leah's cheeks burn, but it also brought a smile to her face.

"Come, let me help you dress." Ginny set down the breakfast tray and bustled over to her side. After Ginny had laced her into the green dress, she braided Leah's hair into one long, fat braid. Then, Ginny handed her a white square of cloth and helped Leah tied it under her chin – this must be the wimple-thing she'd mentioned before. It felt odd to wear, but the servingmaid made approving noises in her throat.

Leah hadn't taken more than a few bites of her breakfast when Ginny wrung her hands impatiently. "Hurry, my lady, or we'll be late. Father Andrew insisted you should be there this morning, if you were up to it."

Late? Late for what?

This was one of those times that Leah really wished for her voice. Cramming a decidedly unladylike portion into her mouth, she followed behind the servant down the maze of corridors in the castle.

Much to her surprise, Ginny led her through the castle, across the courtyard, and into a small stone building on the far end of the castle. All heads turned when she entered, and she noticed Father Andrew standing at the front of the room, standing before an ornate cross. The women's heads were covered, the same as her own, and their hands clasped at their breasts. The men were neatly groomed, and she noticed Royce had shaved.

Church. Mass. Of course. Today must be Sunday.

Father Andrew looked up and his lips pulled down in a slight frown. Leah felt like a jerk for interrupting mass, and crossed herself quickly, moving to the back of the room and bowing her head in prayer. The priest resumed after a brief moment of silence, beginning to recite in Latin once more. The crowd murmured the appropriate responses and Leah had to settle for crossing herself in response.

Leah found her attention wandering the room as the priest delivered his sermon. No benches or pews adorned the small chapel, which she thought was odd, and it didn't help her legs much when the priest continued to drone on and on. The familiar mermaid ache began to flow up her legs, and she bit her lip, hoping for the service to be over soon. As her gaze focused in on the front of the room, she noticed Royce's bent head was turned toward her. So he was watching her? Leah straightened a little and assumed her most pious expression.

The sermon stretched on until the priest bowed his head, intoning a final, "Amen." The crowd chorused after him and then began to disperse. Worried that Lady Matilda would see her and start another scene, Leah grabbed her skirts and hurried out of the small chapel.

"Leah, I would see you a moment please, my child." Father Andrew's placid voice called to her across the chapel, just before she could get out the door.

Curses. Caught like a rat in a trap. She turned slowly, forcing her fisted hands to unclench from her skirt, and pasting the sweetest smile possible on her face. *Keep calm. Remember what Muffin said. You're here for a second chance at life, not to fight over a guy.* Leah turned her most gracious, most innocent face to the priest.

"You allow your whore to come to mass?" Lady Matilda's sugary voice became a screech. "Is nothing sacred in this keep? When I am mistress—"

"When you are mistress," Royce interjected smoothly, "you will still have no say in the matter. Are we quite clear?"

Matilda's face turned a mottled shade of purple.

Leah had to bite her cheek even harder to keep from smiling. She turned her serene gaze to Father Andrew and made a gesture with her hand that he should continue.

The priest seemed a bit disconcerted. "It is a matter that requires... delicacy, lady. I think it would be best discussed in private."

Her gaze slid to Lady Matilda, then back to the priest.

"I'm afraid it will have to wait, Father." Royce moved to her side and grasped her elbow in his hand, his grip unyielding. His eyes were flinty as he stared down at her. "I have things I wish to discuss with Leah that cannot wait."

As Leah watched, Matilda picked up her skirts and lifted her chin, storming out of the chapel with as much dignity as possible. So much for that. She turned to glance at Royce and found him staring down at her, an unreadable look on his face.

He grabbed her by the elbow again and began to pull her out of the chapel.

"Wait, my lord," Father Andrew pleaded. "I need to speak to her."

"It can wait," Royce growled and continued to drag Leah across the courtyard. "I'll send her back to you once we're done."

All eyes turned to stare at them at that statement, and Leah flushed bright red. That certainly didn't leave much to the imagination, and her temper flared at the indignity. She tried to jerk away from him, but his fingers were firm on her arm as he propelled her forward.

Royce escorted her down a hall and through the great hall of the castle. She recognized where they were – her own bedroom was near here. But he didn't stop there. Rather, he continued on to the far end of the corridor, where he opened a door and pushed her inside.

Leah stumbled in, her legs tangling in her skirts, furious at him. How dare he treat her like this?

A female servant was in the room, picking up clothing. At the sight of Royce and Leah, she stopped in her tracks, her mouth falling open in surprise. "Please leave us, Mary." His voice was solicitous and kind. "I have things I wish to say to Leah."

As she watched, the servant nodded and scurried out of the room with the laundry. He shut the heavy door and bolted it, then turned back to her.

Leah took a step backward at the cold look in his eyes. She bumped against something hard, sending a shockwave of sensation up her ultra-sensitive legs. A quick glance behind her revealed the hard item to be a bed. A very large, very masculine bed.

She was in Royce's room.

Her heart hammered in her throat, and she glanced back at Royce in surprise. Why was she in his room?

He was still staring at her with that icy glare, approaching her slowly. "Cease with the innocent act, woman." His body butted up against her own, and she could feel the anger and heat radiating from him. His fingers brushed along her cheek, as if testing the quality of her skin. "So beautiful. I see why Rutledge must have prized you so."

She froze, her spirits taking a downward plunge. She tried to brush his fingers away.

He gripped her chin in his hand, forcing her to look up into his eyes. "I want to know why you've lied to me."

Lied to him? Lied to him about what?

His cold gray eyes stared down into her own. "I want to know where you were last night, Leah."

She stilled in his arms, then tried to break free of his overwhelming embrace. His arm snaked around her waist, pulling her closer and pressing her body against his. Trapping her there.

Panic snaked through her. How much had he seen? How much did he know? Had he seen her on the beach last night?

"I see the guilt in your eyes," he said. "Did you not think that I'd go to your room last night? To comfort you? To explain myself when I've vowed to seduce you and my betrothed shows up on my doorstep? You may be just a leman, Leah, but even I have compassion. I imagined you sitting all alone in your tower room, crying to yourself, and went to you." His fingers brushed against her cheek again, then dropped. "Imagine my surprise when you were not there."

Leah flinched and looked away.

"I thought perhaps that you had gone to the jakes. So I waited. And waited. And when you did not return in an hour, I left." His voice became hard. "And I want to know, my sweet Leah, where you were."

Startled, Leah stared up at him and shook her head. How could she explain?

"Did you kiss him, Leah? Did you kiss him freely while I must fight for every kiss from your lips?" His hands slid around her face, cupping her cheeks and forcing her to look up at him again. His eyes were stormy, revealing the torment inside. "Did he taste the sweetness of your mouth and now he can't get you out of his mind?" His thumb slid across her lip, and his eyes focused there.

A shiver crept across her flesh, and her breath began to quicken at his touch. She closed her eyes and leaned into the caress.

He groaned, his hand sliding down to her ass and pressing her against the junction of his hips. "I want you, Leah. You know this. I've never lied to you about what I want." He bent his head close to her own, his mouth skimming along the edge of her jaw, teasing at her throat. "What I don't understand is what you want. You can't speak, but your eyes tell me that you want me, too — but every time I touch you, you tense up like a scared virgin."

His lips found the shell of her ear and she felt his teeth gently tug on the sensitive skin, teasing her into mindlessness. A soft moan escaped her.

It excited him. He pulled her hips against his own, squeezing at her buttocks. "That's it, Leah," he breathed into her ear. "Let me touch you. Let me wipe those other men out of your mind. You're mine."

She stiffened against him at his words, struggling to break free of his grip.

He ignored her struggles, his head dipping against her throat. She could feel his mouth on her skin, and he sucked, hard. It shot a thrill through her body, and her fisted hands unclenched, and then clenched again, this time against his shoulders. Her body loosened against his.

Slowly her hands un-fisted and she clung to the front of his tunic, angling her face toward his. His lips brushed hers once more and then he pulled away, as if waiting to see her response to him.

Leah wasn't ready for the kiss to be over. She tugged on the neck of his tunic, jerking his face back down to hers and planting her mouth firmly against his. Teeth clashed and her lips felt bruised, but she didn't care. The only thing that mattered was his mouth on hers.

When she reached up to continue the kiss, he groaned against her lips and leaned into her. His tongue delved into her mouth in a slow, hypnotic rhythm, and he ground his hips against hers with each thrust. She wanted to sink against him and be absorbed into his skin, part of him forever.

He lifted her hips up against his once more, and then he was lifting her back onto the bed, nudging her legs apart and resting his knee between them. His lips left hers and she felt his hand roam away from her buttocks to her thigh, stroking her leg and easing her skirts up. Her breath quickened and her eyes slid open at this new, dangerous angle to their embrace, and found him watching her with narrowed eyes as he laid her back on the bed. "Do you want me to touch you, Leah?"

She wanted it very much, she realized. The barest brush of his hand against her skin was doing wild things to her mind, and when his fingers skimmed along the inside of her thigh, her whole body clenched in anticipation. She arched her back toward him, indicating that yes, she would like very much to be touched.

Royce's fingertips slid up her knee, then skimmed her thigh. Closer and closer he came to the hot, throbbing spot she wanted him to touch more than anything, the thought of which was making her mindless. "Do you, Leah?"

She nodded, her hands sliding over the shoulders of his tunic, her eyes closed as she swam in the sensations.

"Then ask me for it."

Her eyes flew open. Humiliated, she tugged her skirts back down around her legs and slapped his hands away, then leapt off the bed and shoved past him. Tears of embarrassment and hurt flooded her eyes, but she averted her face. She didn't want him to see that he'd hurt her.

He didn't follow her. "If you want me, Leah, I'll be waiting for you. But you'll have to make the first move." Royce's voice was wintry in its arrogance.

Leah didn't look behind her. Instead, she tore out of the room and down the hallway, seeking refuge in her own bedroom.

And as luck would have it, Lady Matilda was coming down the hall, accompanied by one of her ladies. She stared at Leah, her eyes growing narrow when she noticed the room that Leah was leaving.

Leah didn't care. She slammed the bedroom door shut behind her.

Chapter Twelve

After that, Matilda seemed to realize she had the upper hand.

Leah hid in her small bedroom for the majority of the day. She skipped dinner that night. She didn't want to face Lady Matilda's gloating face, didn't want to see Royce's accusing eyes. Someone knocked at her door sometime during the evening, but she ignored it, huddling under the covers and feeling miserable.

It was obvious – Royce wasn't in love with her. She couldn't make him fall in love with her if he mistrusted her. Worst of all, she couldn't defend her honor, so he suspected her guilt by way of her silence. He was probably toasting his engagement to Lady Matilda even now.

She was doomed.

Hunger made her get dressed the next morning, though she felt dull and exhausted despite the many hours of sleep. Her legs throbbed – she'd skipped her nightly journey to the beach, terrified at getting caught – and she had the twinges of pain with every step as a result. Ginny hadn't made her usual morning appearance – either Royce had scared her off or Matilda had, so Leah laced up her dress, finger-combed her hair, and headed for the great hall.

It was a mistake. The hall was nearly empty, with the room emptying out as the food trenchers were carried away by servants. Most of Royce's soldiers had gotten up and left, and all that remained were a few lone stragglers, some servants, and Lady Matilda and her crew at the head table.

Leah flinched at the sight of them. Just what she needed.

A catlike smile spread across Lady Matilda's features when she noticed Leah. The woman was dressed immaculately, as usual, with an elegant two-pointed hat perched atop her head, covered in gold veils. They made her blue eyes stand out, even when they were narrowed in hate.

The woman gave Leah a quick up and down look, as if assessing her competition. The triumphant smile that spread across her face told that she found Leah clearly lacking.

Leah's appetite died anew at the sight of her, and she turned to leave.

"Oh, Leah, do come here. I've something I wish to discuss with you." Lady Matilda's overly sweet voice rang across the hall. "It concerns your status in this household."

That was the last thing Leah wanted to discuss. She hesitated, torn between confronting Matilda and turning tail and bolting out of the room. The smirk on Matilda's face spoke volumes. Had Royce confirmed her as his fiancée and she wished to brag over it? Leah's heart sank at the thought.

Before she could decide, a hand slid under her elbow. "Leah," said Father Andrew, at her side. "Do you have time to have that discussion we mentioned?"

Grateful for the interruption, she let him guide his hand to the loop of her arm and turned with him, nodding. Saved by the kindness of the priest. Leah smiled at him, relieved.

"I do apologize, Lady Matilda, but my discussion with Leah cannot wait." He spoke soothingly to the woman. "I have matters of grave importance that we must discuss."

"See that you work harder at saving her soul, father," Matilda replied tartly as she nibbled on a piece of pastry. "Whoring is not a becoming trade."

"Of course, my lady." Father Andrew took Leah's arm and gently steered her away, out of the main hall.

They met Royce on the way out, and Leah flinched again. It was really turning out to not be her day. She averted her gaze and would not look at him.

All he said was, "Greetings, Father. I trust you are well."

"Indeed," came the mild reply. "If you will excuse me, my lord, Leah and I have business to attend to."

"I see."

Leah watched Royce's feet step aside, and Father Andrew began to guide her forward again. "It will be all right," the priest said, patting her hand. "Trust me in this."

At least someone had faith in things.

Royce scowled as he entered the great hall. It had been a trying day already. He'd found one of his guardsmen dead, and a good deal of coin stolen from his stores. He hadn't slept much last night due to Leah's deceptions; he'd gone to bed hard as a stone and been unable to sleep. He'd even knocked at Leah's door last night to try and talk to her, but when she didn't answer his temper got the better of him again. He imagined her locked in the arms of her secret lover, and went to bed furious.

Seeing her in the great hall just made it worse. He remembered the way she'd looked yesterday on his bed, all soft and warm under his hands. He remembered the pleased, surprised look of pleasure on her face when he touched the inside of her creamy thigh. Hell, he was getting hard just thinking about it.

And he remembered the look of hurt that flashed across her expressive face when he'd told her to beg.

He was right.

She was just a whore who was trying to capture her new master... so why did he feel like such a knave?

He turned to Lady Matilda, whose smug face was beginning to grate on his nerves, and sighed. His future was looking grim indeed.

Women's feelings, he thought with annoyance. Distracting him from the real problems in his keep. The traitor in their midst was still at large. Someone was still on Baron Rutledge's side, stealing for him. Attacking his men.

And all he could think about were a pair of green eyes in a sad face.

Hell.

Father Andrew led her to the chapel and pulled out a couple of stools for them to sit on while they talked. Her legs flared with pain when she bent her knees, but she smoothed her skirts and feigned a smile when he sat down next to her.

Leah nodded uncomfortably.

He smiled, but the smile did not reach his warm brown eyes. "I wanted to talk to you today... in regards to a few things. Did you finish the sewing I left for you? The townsfolk will be quite pleased to have the clothing back and whole again. The poor need so much."

Well, shoot. She'd completely forgotten about that. Leah winced and shook her head, an apologetic frown on her face. She gestured, trying to indicate that she'd get it done as soon as possible.

"I see." Father Andrew looked disappointed. "Well, if you will give it back to me, I'll find if one of the other castle women has time. I just thought..."

Leah touched his hand and shook her head. She made a sewing motion with her hands – she'd get on that basket and finish it tonight.

"Thank you, Leah. It means a lot to me that you'd do this."

She nodded, feeling like a jerk. She'd been so wrapped up in her own problems that she'd completely forgotten about the charity work she'd promised to do.

"I find myself... concerned about the state of the castle." He leaned forward and clasped her hands in his own, a grave look on his face. "I have heard whispers and rumors that all is not well within. I know you cannot speak, but I wonder if perhaps others say things near you and discount the fact that you cannot talk. Tell me, have you heard the people speak of a rebellion against Lord Royce's rule? Do they want the old Baron back?"

Leah's eyes widened. Royce was in danger? She shook her head at the priest mutely, wishing she knew more about the subject. She hadn't heard a thing, which relieved her and worried her at the same time.

"I see," Father Andrew said, releasing her hands and leaning back, a thoughtful look on his face. "The reason why I bring this up, Leah... the arrow you took in your arm. It was not the only incident."

It wasn't?

"I have heard... some of Lord Royce's men have been attacked. Funds have been stolen from him. Livestock has been killed. Someone is waging a silent war on him in the name of Baron Rutledge, and I fear for Royce's safety. I think you should stay away from him for the next few days, Lady Leah. Let him be distracted by Lady Matilda and her money, and keep yourself safe. I fear for your safety and do not want you to be harmed." He stood, his gentle eyes full of concern.

Woodenly, she stood as well. Her head spun. He thought Royce was in enough danger to warrant warning her away from him? She had to talk to Muffin. Something was very wrong about the whole situation. She nodded absently, then gave the priest a clumsy curtsy, made all the more stiff and painful by the fire that shot through her legs.

She had to see Royce.

But first, the beach.

Leah didn't waste any time, racing through the empty passageway and shucking her clothes. The shore was chilly and her body shivered with the cold. She didn't stay in the water for long – the peace of being a mermaid was not with her today.

Muffin was nowhere to be seen, either. After a disappointing hour of waiting, Leah headed back to the keep before she caught a cold. Her room was empty, just as she'd left it, and she changed into a new, clean gown, braided her wet hair, then headed for the solar. She could at least sew the clothes she promised while she tried to sort the thoughts in her mind. She longed to find Royce, to run her hands over his shoulders and make sure that he was well. She wanted to tell him what the priest had said to her and confess her fears to him.

She couldn't, though. He was angry at her, and she was still cursed to be a half-fish mute. She wished she could tell Royce the truth – that she wasn't silent because she was his enemy. She was silent because her fairy godmother was crazy (though that sounded ridiculous, too).

In the solar, though, she couldn't seem to keep busy. Her hands fussed idly with the mending, but she ended up dumping it back in the basket and staring out the window-slits instead.

The courtyard was full of people, and, as she watched, several of them rushed to the far end of the courtyard. *Something is happening,* she thought to herself, and panic set in. She couldn't see where they were all rushing to.

Worst of all, she couldn't see Royce.

Leah fled the room, grabbing her skirts in her hands and clattering down the stairs at breakneck speed. Down she raced, through the hallways, through the great hall, outside to the courtyard where she nearly slammed into the back of one of the peasants. They were all crowding around something, and Leah's heart hammered in her throat. Something was wrong.

Please, please Muffin, she thought. *Don't let it be Royce. Let him be well. Let him be safe.*

She pushed her way through the crowd and stared down at the scene before her. A figure lay on the ground, covered in mud and blood. A knife lay in a puddle next to him, and everyone whispered, staring and pointing at the body.

The body was not Royce's. Leah burst into relieved tears at the sight, putting her hand to her mouth and biting her knuckles to muffle the noisy sobs that threatened to erupt.

"Leah?" Across the crowd, Royce came to her. His tunic was ripped in one part, and blood splashed across the front of his breast.

Her heart nearly stopped again and she surged forward, her fingers ripping at the fabric to check the wound. Tears poured down her face, mixing with the rain, and her breath came in sharp, harsh little gasps. He'd been hurt – they'd been trying to hurt him.

Father Andrew was right after all.

"All is well, Leah," he soothed, even as her frantic hands searched his chest. His hand brushed her cheek gently. "He managed naught but a scratch. Everything's fine."

Oh. Well. She felt a little silly, throwing herself all over him in the middle of a crowded courtyard with everyone staring at them. Leah snatched her hands back and blushed bright red. Foolish she might look, but Royce was staring at her with the seductive half-grin on his face that she well recognized and that made parts of her anatomy tingle.

Her foot went cold as she stood there, smiling up at Royce. The cold water from the puddle she stood in slicked between her toes, having soaked through one of her slippers. As she felt the wet skin slide and her toes begin to tingle and burn, she realized she was in more danger than she thought.

When a large raindrop splatted atop her head, she realized that between the mud and the rain, it could be enough to begin a change. Fear trumped her concern over Royce, and Leah turned and ran, shoving through the crowd.

"Leah!" Royce called behind her. "Leah, wait!"

She couldn't wait. Stumbling on feet that burned with unholy fire, she raced for the inside of the castle. If she could make it to her room, she'd be safe. No, wait. Her solar was closer. *Go there*, she thought, turning down one corridor and feeling the slap of her wet skirts against her legs. Each step was like stepping on pins and needles, and agonizing jolts of pain lanced up her legs, caught on the verge of transformation.

The solar seemed to take forever to reach, but finally the hard wood of the door was beneath her palms, and she stumbled inside, slamming it shut behind her. Her wet shoes that were causing the transformation flew across the room with two awkward kicks. She rested against the door, her back pressed against it, her breath gasping and heaving as she waited for the pain to subside. A few more minutes, and then she'd be all right. The excruciating tingling and clenching of the bones in her feet was already slowing.

"What are you doing here?"

Leah stifled the groan of frustration that threatened to escape and opened one eye. Sure enough, the hateful woman was staring back at her, affronted. Two of her ladies sat nearby, eyeing Leah with the same prudish expressions.

She straightened against the door, trying to think of a way to explain her actions. Not that she could explain, but she was soaked, she'd burst into the room, slammed the door, and kicked her shoes off. Not exactly the normal actions of your everyday village doxy. So she pasted a bright smile on her face. Maybe she could collect her shoes and leave again before Matilda had time to process everything.

There was a knock at the door, just behind Leah's back. She could feel the vibrations through her ribs. "Leah," Royce called. "Are you well? Is everything all right?"

Lady Matilda's eyes narrowed and her arms crossed over her chest. "What is going on?" Her voice was deadly soft. "What do you think you're doing with my betrothed, *whore*?"

Oh boy.

The door pushed her forward, and Leah stumbled in a few steps as Royce opened the door. "Leah, I—" The words died in his throat when he spotted Matilda's angry face. "Lady Matilda. I did not realize you were in here."

"Obviously," she sneered.

He cleared his throat and eyed Leah, his eyes caressing her as he looked her up and down. Silly, foolish, beautiful man. He was checking to make sure she was ok. A swell of love shot through her.

"I see. Well, I will leave you ladies to yourselves." He sounded as awkward as she felt and shut the door behind him quietly.

The two women stared at each other for a moment. Lady Matilda opened her mouth to say something, but Leah wasn't paying attention anymore. She gathered her shoes calmly, even as Matilda began to screech and rant, and exited the solar.

A quick glance down the hallway showed her that Royce's door shut mere moments after she stepped out. No doubt he was going to change, she thought, remembering his bloody doublet.

So she followed him into his room.

The door was unlocked. She opened it a crack and then slid inside, shutting the door behind her and sliding the latch-lock.

Royce stood in the middle of the room, near the front of the fire. "Leah?" His deep, sensual voice held a note of surprise.

His bare chest dominated her view. All she could do was stare—at the muscles before her face, and the long, deep scratch that crossed his breast. Someone had tried to kill him. They'd tried to kill Royce, and if they'd succeeded, he'd be dead.

Dead like her.

And then she wouldn't get her second chance.

For some reason, that thought frightened her a lot less than imagining Royce bleeding to death under an assassin's knife. She threw down her shoes and stalked across the large chamber toward him. She stopped right in front of Royce, staring up into his beautiful, harsh face. A muffled sob escaped her lips and she shook her head and closed her eyes, frustrated at her inability to communicate.

"Hush, Leah," his warm fingers stroked her cheek, then her neck. "Everything will be well."

She shook her head, trying to give him a watery smile as she took the edge of her skirt and pressed it against the welling blood. He was hurt, and she felt somehow responsible. If she'd stayed at his side...

She'd gone and fallen in love with the impossible man. And she couldn't even tell him.

He brushed a wet strand of hair off her cheek. "'Tis naught but a scratch, Leah. He wasn't successful. You are working yourself up over nothing." He touched the sleeve of her gown. "You're soaked, and you'll catch a fever. Go and change; I'll be fine." His words were low and husky and sent shivers through her body.

The scratch had stopped bleeding, and she dropped the hem of her skirt. But she didn't leave. Her fingers stretched out and touched his chest, gently exploring the bronzed expanse. He was a large man, a few inches taller than her lanky height, but his shoulders were impossibly broad. His stomach and arms were corded with muscle. Every inch of him was hard.

She heard him suck in his breath at the touch of her fingertips. "Leah," he said, his voice a warning. "Do not tease me." His hand dropped from her face. "If you want me, then show me, but don't torment me. You know how I feel."

Her fingers continued to explore the hard ridges of his abdomen. There was a myriad of scars tracing his skin, some old, some new. He'd mentioned a hard life, and they were proof of that. She snagged her fingers around the edge of his trousers and pulled him closer to her, angling her face toward his, offering herself.

His mouth descended on hers and he pulled her close to him. The feel of his hard body along hers made her toes curl with desire. His teeth found her lower lip and he gently nipped at it, then sucked, and the result was a shockwave of pleasure. Leah melted against him, her hands snaking over his smooth, hard shoulders to twine in his damp hair. Her lips met his again and she kissed him, her tongue dancing with his. The scratch of his beard stubble against her cheek was rough, but added to the edge of excitement.

His teeth gently bit along her lower lip again and moved to her jaw, trailing kisses along her neck. "Do you know how long I've wanted to hold you, Leah?" His hands slid up her back. "To take you in my arms and make you mine?" Royce's hands slid to her laces and she felt him tug them loose. "I want to see every inch of this white skin against my own."

She felt her dress loosen and obediently lifted her arms when he tugged on the fabric, lifting it over her head. The heavy, soaked overdress was gone, leaving her in her thin sherte, which was fine enough to see through. His hands skimmed over her shoulders as if smoothing her, examining her. She slid her hands over his chest, wanting to touch him, to show him that she wanted this as much as he did.

Warm hands stroked across the front of her sherte, moving across her belly and gliding over the hard tips of her breasts. Leah sucked in her breath at the hint of a touch, her eyes going to Royce's. His gray eyes were dark as he stared down at her, hot with desire.

"You're trembling," he said, and brushed a lock of hair back off her shoulder.

She was? She didn't realize. Suddenly self-conscious, she crossed her arms over her chest and shivered. She didn't feel cold. Leah stepped closer to him, slipping her hands around his waist and pulling her body close against his. She heard him inhale as her stomach touched the hard erection just underneath his breeches.

With a low groan, Royce grabbed her under the legs and lifted her into his arms, striding toward the bed and dropping her in there. "God's wounds, woman, but you're a heavy wench."

That broke the thick, almost awkward tension in the room. Leah giggled, reaching up to smack him on the shoulder. He stared down at her, the half-smile frozen on his face, and she sobered. "You're lovely when you smile, Leah. I wish you'd smile more often for me."

She bit her lip and smiled shyly up at him, dazzled by the attention he was showering on her. A girl could get used to this – she felt pampered, beautiful. Special.

"Come, Leah. Show me that beautiful body of yours." He offered her his hand and she took it, letting him pull her into a sitting position atop his massive bed.

Suddenly struck with shyness, she clutched at the collar of her loose sherte, and he chuckled. "Do not play the shy virgin with me now, Leah. We've tortured each other for too long." He slid his hands over her legs, where the dress was rucked up around her knees, and eased it forward. "I want to see your beautiful white flesh," he said, kissing at her neck. "Your long, long legs that are going to be wrapped around me as I bury myself deep inside you."

His words were like a sensual balm, and she obediently let him lift the last remaining article of clothing off of her body and slowly raised her eyes to his.

His eyes were dark with desire. "Lovely," he said, reaching out with one darkly tanned hand to brush against the tip of her breast. The nipple puckered in response, and Leah clutched at his forearms at the jolt of sensation that tore through her. The feeling was intense, almost frightening, if it weren't for the shock of pleasure that had centered through her.

"Your breasts are perfect," he murmured, watching as the other nipple tightened. "Just the right size for my hand." He cupped one and flicked his thumb over the pink crown, his eyes locking onto hers.

Leah gave a sigh of pleasure in response and arched against his hand. That felt... exquisite. She wanted more.

He released her, though, and slid into bed next to her, still dressed in his breeches. Leah lay back on the bed, watching him expectantly. Would he undress and show her the rest of his magnificent body? Was he large all over? She blushed at the thought. Modern women weren't supposed to be such ninnies when it came to sex, but here she was, giggling internally at the thought.

She stopped laughing when his hand stroked her breast, his fingers teasing her nipple. The world tilted at the touch. Sliding her hands over to his chest again, her fingertips brushed against his nipple, exploring. Her eyes went to his, as if seeking approval.

Royce groaned, and he leaned over her, burying his face against her breasts. "God help me, Leah, but you are so beautiful. You make me mad with wanting you, with your pale skin and staring up at me with those big eyes." He nuzzled against her breast and she squirmed underneath him, arching against his face. His chin abraded the tender skin between her breasts, but it was a curious mix of pain and anticipatory pleasure. If he would just put his mouth in the right spot...

Her breath nearly exploded from her when he did. Royce's lips closed over one nipple and gently rolled it between his teeth, and Leah's fingers dug into his shoulders, her breathing escalating. He nipped at her and chuckled. "Like that, do you?"

She flexed her fingers against his shoulders in response, then pressed her breast back against his lips. She wanted more.

He needed no more encouragement, and the sensitive tip of her breast was again enveloped by his lips— stroking, teasing, sucking gently. Leah's hands frantically moved against his body, her fingernails digging into his skin as sensation drove over her. It felt so good, and yet made her so restless.

His hand slid up her leg as he tormented her, and, to Leah, the sensations suddenly tripled in power. He leaned half-over her in the immense bed, his mouth making love to her breasts, his hand sliding up between her legs and sending little thrilling shockwaves reverberating through her body as she twined her fingers in his hair and gasped and panted like she couldn't breathe.

And then his hot, scalding hand touched the flesh at the junction of her thighs and her body went into overdrive.

She panicked, her thighs clenching at the onslaught of feeling, and darted away from him on the bed. *Stupid, stupid* she told herself. *Don't be such an idiot. He thinks you're experienced. You're supposed to be experienced.*

But it was happening a little faster than she could handle. Instead, she pulled his face up to hers and dove to his mouth for another long, sweet, lingering kiss.

"Nay, sweet one," he breathed against her mouth, and she felt his hand slide between her clamped thighs once more. "Let me touch you. Look at me, Leah," he coaxed, and slid one hot finger through her folds. She did, and nearly drowned in his gray eyes. "Let me worship your body, like it should be."

He didn't have to, she wanted to protest. She liked what he was doing already very much, and she didn't feel like she was doing enough. But then he touched the nub of her, and she lost track of her thoughts entirely. She gasped at the sensation when he rubbed it slowly, and her body grew wild with the slow, teasing, torturous touch. Her gasps turned to whimpers as her hips clenched against his hand and she bucked against him, her lips frantically seeking his and biting at his lower lip, desperate to find an outlet for the frantic sensation that was building up inside of her.

He jerked away when she bit too hard, though she could tell he was pleased by the way she was writhing beneath him. "Slow down, Leah. We have time." He slid lower, pressing his lips down her abdomen, moving his face down her body.

It didn't feel like it – her body wanted release, and it wanted it *now*.

And it came an instant later, the moment he parted her nether lips and his mouth touched the most sensitive part of her body. Everything seemed to explode at once in mindless pleasure, escaping her through a low, frantic keen and shudder after shudder of pleasure.

Her body was slow to calm – the immediate aftershocks rippled through her, followed by a languid pleasure that was almost as enjoyable as what just happened. Her eyes opened slowly, and she looked down at Royce, nestled at the junction of her thighs, not moving, just watching her and waiting.

"Are you back with me now?" His voice was low and husky, throbbing with unspent passion, and she realized he hadn't come to the same shattering release she had.

She nodded slowly, resisting the urge to stretch against him. Her body began to quiver anew at the hungry look he gave her. Royce planted a kiss at the apex of her thighs and slid up on the bed, slowly covering her.

He leaned in for another hungry kiss, his hard body sliding against her own, and she felt pleasure stir through her again when she felt his hard chest against her nipples. Her hands slid over his back, wanting to pull him so far against her that they'd become one.

His thigh nudged hers apart, and no more coaxing was needed. She slid her legs around his waist, and it felt natural. His hard, hot member pressed against the wet triangle between her legs, and she sucked in her breath as an entirely new set of sensations rocked through her. He rocked against her, rubbing, his eyes locked with hers, testing her readiness.

The rubbing was driving her nearly mad with desire. Leah groaned when he slid his hard cock between her slick folds again, lifting her hips in suggestion. There was a bone-deep ache between her legs, and she wanted him there to fill it.

"Do you want this as much as I do, Leah?" He rubbed against her again. "If not, let me know and I'll stop." His words were gritted between his teeth.

She reached up and touched his cheek gently, letting him know that she wanted it as well, raising her hips against his.

With a groan, he shifted her in his arms, and she felt the tip of his cock nudging against her, seeking. She didn't have time to dwell on this for more than a moment and then he was inside her in one deep thrust, and the sudden, sharp pain made her suck in her breath.

He stilled on top of her. "Leah?" Royce's body became rigid, and then he swore. "You're a virgin?"

She shook her head at him, urging him on. The pain was still there, stretching and testing, and she wanted nothing more to squirm away... except she wasn't supposed to be a virgin. Leah smiled faintly up at him.

He began to pull away from her. "God's bones, woman—"

She trapped him against her, wrapping her legs around him. He paused, then looked down at her. She shook her head at him, reaching to pull him down against her and take his lips in another hot, sensual kiss. Again, she lifted her hips against his, feeling the twinge of pain again, but not as strong as before. The stretching sensation was a unique one… one that she wanted to experience more of, pain or no pain. She sucked on his lower lip, suggestively.

He groaned again, as if it was too much for him, and rocked into her once more, nearly lifting her off the bed with the force of it. Again, she gasped against his lips, but the pain was nearly gone, replaced by a curious, filled longing that she wanted more of. He thrust again, and again, his mouth sliding down to capture hers in a brief, ardent kiss between each thrust.

Between each sensual kiss and each piercing thrust, Leah began to feel that slow urgency build up in her body again. Her responses became more frenzied.

It was all the encouragement he needed; Royce leaned into her and began to thrust faster and harder, and she lifted up to welcome each hard, swift entry into her body. The world began to blend and haze around her, and nothing existed but Royce's body against hers and the sensations between them. She whimpered against him, her nails digging into his back.

With one quick touch, he teased the tip of her breast and thrust into her again, leaning forward and grinding his hips against her own in a slow, sensual thrust. She slid apart at that moment in a gasping cry, her body clenching around him as she found release once more.

It seemed to drive him over the edge, as well. With a few more sharp, hard thrusts, before her body could even come down from the ebb of pleasure it was on, he groaned and tensed against her, and she felt his body spasm against hers. Then he groaned her name and collapsed on top of her.

They lay like that for long moments, both panting and skin dewy with sweat. Leah enjoyed the feel of him on top of her, hearing his heart strum against her own. This was the most perfect place to be in the world at the moment – against his skin, smelling his sweat, his body melded with hers.

He moved off of her too soon for her own liking, rolling to the side of the bed. Disappointment shot through her, only to be tamped when he reached over and pulled her against him. She brushed a sweaty lock of hair off of his brow and smiled shyly at him.

Royce didn't smile back. "How is it that Lord Rutledge's leman is a virgin?"

She stiffened against him and tried to escape, but his arms held her captive. His eyes searched hers, his mouth drawn into a grim line. "Answers Leah, I need answers."

She couldn't give him answers. Frustrated, she pointed at his softening erection and made a crass gesture, indicating that her 'supposed' lover couldn't muster enough enthusiasm.

A startled look flashed across Royce's face, followed by a chuckle. "Now that's something I never considered." His arms tightened around her. "Am I the only man that's touched you like that?" His voice took on a husky note.

Her own breathing quickened at his words, and she nodded against his chin.

Her response pleased him, and he rolled her beneath him once more, a wicked grin on his face. "Lucky for you, wench, that I do not suffer the same problem as Rutledge."

Leah giggled with delight.

Chapter Thirteen

The sun rose too early the next day to suit Leah. Royce's chamber had no windows, but she could see light seeping in through the arrow slit and she groaned, rolling over in the large bed and snuggling up against his large, warm body. He put a hand on her hip in response and kissed her neck.

The hand on her hip sent a shockwave of pain lancing through her and she flinched.

He didn't seem to notice, and pulled her against him, cushioning her head on his chest. "I'd best get up soon, wench. There's a lot to do today – the men need training. We've got to keep on our guard for when Baron Rutledge counter-attacks and tries to take Northcliffe back." His arms tightened around her. "Much as I'd love to spend all day in bed with you, I'd best get out." He pressed a kiss on her forehead and rolled out of bed.

She propped up on her side and watched him dress. There were more scars on his back, one a long gouge down his shoulder and crossing down his back toward one firm, muscled buttock. Leah blushed when she realized she was staring at his ass. The man was gorgeous clothed, but he was even more stunning naked.

Royce turned and grinned at her. "Keep looking at me like that, Leah, and I'll forget all about my men, and rejoin you in the bed."

She grinned and wiggled her eyebrows at him suggestively, tracing a finger on the bedspread.

He was back at the edge of the bed in an instant, leaning over her and kissing her fiercely enough to make her toes curl. Leah's tongue stroked against his, and she gave a sigh of happiness when he pulled away, smiling up at him.

He grinned down at her and kissed the tip of her nose. "I have to go. Why don't you head down to the kitchens and see what cook's got to eat? If I had to wager a guess, I'd guess that we've missed the morning meal."

They had? Oh lord, both of them? Leah's nerves suddenly stretched taut. Lady Matilda wouldn't have liked that very much. When Royce stepped away from the bed to get a clean tunic, Leah sat up in bed and swung her legs over the side experimentally. A slight throb of pain here and there, but she was almost getting used to the constant aching by now. With luck, she'd be able to get down to the beach sometime today.

He helped her dress quickly in her over-garment, now wrinkled and smelling musty, and laced the sides while she finger-combed her hair. Hopefully, Leah reasoned, no one would be down their particular hall of the castle at this time of day, and she could sneak into her room and fix her appearance enough to where she didn't look... well, obvious.

He finished tying the laces and moved her tangled hair aside to kiss her neck. "You still smell like pleasure," he whispered against her skin, which caused a little ripple of delight to thrum through her body. "Regretfully, I can't stay the day in bed with you, but you'll come back to me tonight?"

Leah nodded, flushing with color. Her mind raced. If he wanted her to spend every night with him, how was she going to get down to the beach? She'd have to figure out a way.

When he opened the door to his chambers, however, he found a surprise.

Lady Matilda stood there, dressed in her finery, staring at the both of them with hate in her eyes. Two of her women stood behind her, the bored looks sliding off their faces as soon as the door opened. Her pretty blue eyes were narrowed into slits, her angelic face framed by a white wimple and equally pale gown.

She cocked her head, staring at the two of them, and Leah resisted the urge to step behind Royce's large frame and let him take the brunt of her anger.

She'd completely forgotten about Matilda. And now she'd gone and slept with the woman's fiancée.

That was pretty crappy of her, all things considering.

But Matilda didn't look sad or brokenhearted – she looked furious. "So." She eyed them both, but her gaze focused on Leah, her eyes sweeping over the rumpled dress and bed-hair. "I saw the two of you disappear into this chamber last night, but I had my hopes. I had hoped that my soon-to-be husband would cut his doxy loose and take up the reins of propriety, at least until we were married." Her voice raised an octave, becoming faster and more shrill the longer she spoke. "And then I hear the chambermaids giggling about the two of you locked in there! And the whole castle is talking about how their new Lord Royce has finally conquered his little mute! And I thought surely that they must be wrong, for what man would look at this... this creature," she said, gesturing furiously at Leah, "when I am here?"

Ouch.

Royce cut off Matilda's ranting with a flick of his hand. "You go too far, woman. Your dowry is the only

111

appealing thing about you, and even it pales with every moment spent in your presence."

Lady Matilda's jaw dropped. She huffed, looking as if she was going to inflate, and before she could speak, Royce took Leah by the hand and pulled her past the woman and her covey of maids. "Excuse us."

Leah trotted behind Royce obediently, though she couldn't help glancing back at Matilda. The woman had recovered, her eyes narrowed to slits again, and she was staring at Leah with blatant animosity.

Royce didn't take Leah very far – just the few steps to her room, and caressed her cheek gently when he opened the door. "I'll meet you later and we'll talk more."

She nodded and shut the door gently, wanting to get away from Matilda's accusing stare more than the tender look on Royce's face.

As she shut the door, she heard a screech in the hall behind them. "Talk? You can't talk with that little fool! She's a mute! What could she possibly say to you?"

Leah bolted the door and smiled faintly to herself. She was looking forward to the day when she'd be able to say plenty to Lady Matilda. Turning away from the door, she touched the brick near the fireplace and waited for the secret passage to reveal itself.

She'd need her mermaid time now, if she was planning on meeting up with Royce again tonight. And she didn't intend to let anything interrupt that. A sensual smile curved her lips as she hugged herself, giddy with emotion. She was in love.

Surely he wasn't but a few steps behind her in that matter, if last night were any proof.

Muffin clearly thought otherwise.

The woman had descended upon Leah moments before she was able to shed her skirts and dive into the water. She stared at the tide, feeling it match the ebbing and rising throb in her legs. The pull of it was no match for Muffin's not-so-silent disapproval.

"I can't believe you," she said for the ninth time, fluttering her heavily ringed hands in agitation. "After you've worked so hard to pull this off, you throw it away. Tossed! Vanished! Gone!"

Leah put her hands up protectively, not wanting to be smacked in the chin by the overlarge ruby ring that encircled one of Muffin's fingers. "What are you talking about, Muffin? Things are finally working out." She was actually starting to get pretty confident about the whole thing. Royce would declare his love soon. Then she'd be able to tell Muffin that Royce needed to come with her, back to the modern world, of course – the fairy godmother might be dotty, but she wouldn't be so cruel as to separate the two of them, not when they were both clearly in love. It was all going to work out beautifully.

"Get that dreamy look off your face, girl," Muffin said, her voice snapping with anger. "This is a serious matter."

"Tell me while I'm in the water," Leah pleaded. "My legs hurt so badly I can hardly think straight."

"That much is obvious, judging from last night." The fairy godmother gave a sniff but moved aside. "Very well, hurry on in, child, so we can figure out how to fix this."

Leah rushed for the water, hastily stripping off her clothes. The first kiss of the ocean was frighteningly cold, and she gasped at the sensation. It was like a prickly brush of ice against her skin, only to be replaced by the familiar burning and clenching in her legs as they began the change. She struggled deeper into the water, moving forward until she was in the cold brine up to her neck. Her gills fluttered, chugging the icy cold ocean in and out with each breath.

It was like an immense relief to feel her mermaid form once more, and Leah relaxed in the water, soaking her hair and letting the tide carry her back and forth, her tail flicking. She'd get back to shore soon enough and deal with Muffin's displeasure.

Something hard bumped against her head and she sat up in the water, twisting her tail to keep her balance. Muffin sat there in a small rowboat, clutching a ruffled parasol and dressed in a bathing costume like something from the turn of the century – bright red and blue with culottes. "I think you've messed this one up, girl."

"I haven't." She shook her head, brushing wet, salty locks of hair off her face. "I think I'm closer than ever. He's going to fall in love with me, I just know it."

"No, he won't!" Her voice rose in a shrill crescendo that reminded her oddly of Matilda. "Why would he be interested in the cow if he's getting the milk for free?"

Leah splashed at the boat, her gills heaving furiously with her own irritation. "That's just an old cliché."

"They become clichés for a reason, my dear." The fairy godmother leaned over the boat and glared at her. "Now that he's had your... goodies... you're going to have to work extra hard to keep him attracted to you."

Muffin was wrong. Leah glared at her and resisted the urge to dive back under the dark, calming waters of the ocean. No doubt if she did, Muffin would show up there with a scuba outfit. "Wasn't this what you wanted? You've been pushing and pushing for me to take this to the next level for a while now. And now that I have, you're mad at me? I don't understand." She smacked the side of the boat in frustration. "What do you want from me?"

Muffin shook her head and moved her parasol to her other shoulder as the boat began to rotate in the water. "I am a fairy godmother, girl. A fairy *godmother*. Not a pimp. I told you to encourage him. Tease him. Toss your hair at him a little. Make him want you. Keep him thirsting for more and *don't* give it to him. That's the trick to keeping a man panting after you."

Yeah, because a dotty little old lady was such an expert. Leah resisted the urge to retort something unkind and grabbed the prow of the boat to stop it from spinning around again. Count on Muffin to get one without oars. "He's not going to lose interest, Muffin. I think he's going to fall in love with me."

"If you say so." The woman raised an eyebrow, clearly lacking the faith Leah had. "Most men don't fall in love with their bit on the side. You've gone from an intriguing challenge to an easy conquest, and now he'll lose interest."

That stung. "But I think I'm falling in love with him."

Muffin leaned forward, her parasol blotting out the sun. "And that, my dear, is the biggest problem of all. Do yourself a favor and don't fall in love. It's not going to lead to anything. Understand me? Provided you win this little challenge, you're off to a new mortal life. If you lose, you're on your way to the Afterlife. He can't follow you to either one."

Muffin's words had been harsh, but she'd succeeded in her goal – getting Leah back on track. She needed to make sure that she kept Royce interested in her – and she doubted the best way to do that was to moon after him like the lovesick fool that she was.

She moped about in her rooms for the rest of the afternoon, managing only a few small smiles for cheerful Ginny, who brought a cleaned dress for her and chattered on as if she didn't notice Leah's depression.

When Ginny shooed her out of her bedroom and told her with a sly smile that Royce was awaiting her in the great hall, she went to the solar instead.

The sitting room looked the same as it ever did. The sewing table nearby had a piece of needlework carelessly discarded on it, and the window seat was bare, the last of the daylight lighting it. Leah headed there.

A servant slipped in, bowing to Leah when she turned. "I was told you'd be up here, my lady," he said, giving her a knowing smile that made her blush. "He gave me orders to bring this to you to ease your appetite." The man set down the basket, lit a candle, and left, shutting the door behind him.

Leah's stomach growled and she headed over to the table, hunger getting her past the melancholy. The basket was full of a variety of delicacies. Bits of roasted meat left in a bread trencher, a few pastries, and some dainty circles of cheese. There were even a few small treats that she knew to be apple tarts, and she popped one into her mouth. The flavor was cloyingly sweet, with an annoying aftertaste, and she grimaced. She'd never get used to the medieval custom of over-spicing everything. She ate one more, then moved on to the cheeses, pulling up a stool and beginning to eat. No sense starving herself.

A few minutes later, there was a quick knock at the door and Leah swallowed her last mouthful, staring at the door with wary anticipation. What now?

But it was Royce that stepped into the room, his dark hair tousled and the expression on his face unreadable. "Leah? Why do you hide up here?"

Her stomach twisted into knots at the sight of him. She sat down weakly at the table and offered him a small half-smile. How to explain that she was hiding from the world, and indulging in a pity party?

116

The look on Royce's face turned black. "What's troubling you?" When she wouldn't look him in the eye, he shut the solar door behind him and stalked over to her, leaning over the table. "You weren't upset about it last night, Leah. Not when you were in my arms, making those soft noises in your throat as I stroked in your body."

She averted her eyes and placed the last of her cheese on the table. She was going to be sick, her stomach was so upset. Her whole body tensed and she glanced over at him, feeling flushed and uncomfortable.

He leaned over the table, his face partly furious and partly incredulous. Angry that she was being such a baby. Incredulous that she'd change her mind after last night. His dark eyes stared down at her.

This wasn't what she wanted. Muffin be damned – the fairy godmother's advice had her completely turned around, and now he was in danger of cutting her out of his affections entirely. Leah shook her head and buried her face in her hands, not sure what to think.

His arms were around her in seconds, his lips pressing kisses into her hair. "Leah, Leah," he groaned, pulling her against him and cradling her. "I wish you could tell me what's wrong so I could fix it for you." He stroked her hair away from her face. "You're mine. Do you understand me? Whatever has upset you, I'll fix it."

Her heart began to beat hard in her chest, and she snuggled against him, feeling sleepy and flushed. It felt so good to lie in his arms and let him comfort her. Muffin had been wrong – she didn't need to play hard-to-get with him – she needed to love him as much as she could, and if that didn't work? She'd at least have the memories. Leah lifted her tear-stained face to his for a kiss, feeling languid and warm in his embrace.

He kissed her mouth and then pulled away abruptly, seemingly surprised by her lack of reaction. Leah leaned against him, her limbs feeling slow and tired. Her stomach was still cramping and painful, and her heart was still racing, faster than ever. If she could just concentrate...

"Leah?" Royce said, and the sound was overloud in her sensitive ear. "Are you all right? Leah?"

Her last conscious thought before she slid into the black was that perhaps she was not doing quite as well as she thought.

Chapter Fourteen

Royce stared down at Leah's unconscious form in the middle of his bed. She thrashed every now and then in her sleep, her body shuddering with pain, and the whole time, never said a word, never uttered a sound.

It was the silence that got to him most of all, especially when she curled into a ball around her stomach and huddled, silent tears rolling down her face. And so he waited by her side and held her hand to let her know she was not alone.

"You're sure it's poison?" he asked the leech.

The old man nodded, plucking a few of the bloated creatures off of Leah's pale arm and dropping them into a bowl. "The symptoms are there, my lord. The fever, the belly cramps, the pounding in her chest." He leaned forward and opened the unconscious girl's mouth, and Royce leaned forward to look. "Her tongue is swollen as well. Someone's poisoned her, possibly with a food or a drink."

She'd been alone, eating in the solar when he'd seen her. She'd looked so sad as she'd nibbled on her cheeses and tarts, and had fallen into his arms so limply. She couldn't even tell him what was wrong, and he'd nearly brought the castle down with his roars of outrage.

And now, to find out that someone in his castle – his own demesne – had poisoned his woman? Fury boiled in his blood, fury and a thirst for revenge.

Baron Rutledge was no doubt behind this. He'd found out of Leah's seduction and had his spies poison her. His fingers tightened on hers. He'd find out who the traitor was and make him pay.

"My lord," the leech said, and when he got no response, repeated his words. "My lord, perhaps it would be best to bleed her again in an hour. We need to clear the poisons from her body."

"You've bled her three times already and she looks weaker every time." Royce fixed his cold gaze on the leech. "Perhaps you'd best leave her be."

The man bowed and exited the room. "As you wish."

The little man had no sooner cleared the room than Lady Matilda appeared in the doorway, her face souring at the smell of the sickroom. She was accompanied by two of her ladies in waiting that wore identical looks of displeasure. He wondered if he married her, would they follow into the bedchamber? She was never without them. One of the women carried a basket behind her.

Lady Matilda was dressed in fine garments again, her blond hair hidden by an ornate headdress and her full cheeks flushed with life. Royce experienced a stab of resentment, glancing down at Leah's hollow cheeks and her pale complexion.

"What is she doing here?" Matilda's voice was hard on his nerves, all angry edges. "Why is she in your bed?"

"She is here because she is sick." Royce answered, trying not to run a hand down his face in frustration.

"She is a whore," Lady Matilda insisted, oblivious to the fact that he grew more irritated by the second. "She should be in her own chambers above the kitchens, or wherever it is that whores sleep." The woman swept into the room and stood in front of his fireplace, her long, fur-trimmed skirts flaring out behind her and sweeping across the stone floor. "It doesn't befit you as Lord of Northcliffe to sit here and wait hand and foot on the old lord's castoffs."

Her words enraged him – all the more so because they had a grain of truth. Still, he felt guilty for leading Leah down the path that had caused her to be in the state she was now, and Lady Matilda could do nothing except look at her with uncomfortable disdain.

Which made his senses prick. Why was Matilda so very uncomfortable at the sight of Leah?

Unless... she'd been the one to poison her.

Cold flooded through his veins. He stood. "I'm afraid, Lady Matilda, that I'm going to have to cancel our betrothal." He watched with satisfaction as her jaw dropped in a most unladylike fashion. "I find that we wouldn't suit, and I've no wish to find myself married to a murderer."

"A murderer?" Her voice was a shrill cry. "What are you talking about?"

He gestured at the bed furiously. "Tell me that it wasn't you that poisoned your rival? Can't stand to see the man you've chosen with another woman?"

Her brows furrowed together. "Why would I poison your whore? You can't marry her – she's a common trollop."

The urge to slap her grew with every passing moment. "If you know what's best for you, lady, you'll leave this chamber and this castle behind."

She drew herself up stiffly, her eyes flashing outrage. "How dare you?" She hissed at him, picking up her skirts and sweeping past him. She paused in the doorway, magnificent in her beauty and her finery, if not her spirit. "My father will hear of this, and when he does, he will be furious that you would insult our house so." She gestured at one of her ladies, the one holding the basket.

"If you must know, Lord Royce, I came to warn you of your doxy's duplicity, not to confess any sort of murder." She sneered as she regarded him. "I found this in the solar, stuffed into a basket of her mending."

The waiting-woman hurried forward and dropped the basket at Royce's feet. It was a basket of clothing, and he glared at Matilda, wondering what he'd ever seen in the petty shrew. "It's torn clothing."

"Beneath those rags you'll find a great deal of money," Matilda lifted her nose in the air, staring down at him as if he were dung beneath her silk slippers. "Money that's no doubt missing from your coffers."

How had she known about that? He bent down to pick up the basket and sure enough, a good deal of gold and silver plates were revealed just beneath the cloth. They were the missing items from his treasury. "And you found this?"

She straightened even more. "I did."

"In the solar?" He kept his voice as calm as possible. "Yes."

He dropped the basket at his feet again. "Your games go too far, lady. There's no sense in framing a woman that you intended to kill." He gave her a cold look. "You have one hour to leave these premises or I will drop you in the moat myself."

"You don't believe me?"

"You're the only one with reason enough to try and remove Leah. So no, I don't."

Her cheeks flushed with outrage, and Lady Matilda grabbed her skirts and stormed away, a shrill cry of outrage echoing down the hall. "You'll regret this!"

He had a feeling he wouldn't.

When Leah woke again, the entire world ached. Her mouth was dry, her head pounded, and there were waves of familiar pain radiating outward from her legs.

She slid one eye open experimentally. The room was dark, lit only by a faint, wavering candle behind her. The pillow beneath her cheek was soft and full, the mattress not the hard ticking that hers had been. The blankets brushing her arms were fur. She was in Royce's room, then.

Her mind was fuzzy. Why did everything hurt so much? She rolled over in the bed and nearly cried at the pain that shot through her.

"Leah?" The husky voice was at her side, full of concern, and she focused her eyes in on Royce's shadowed face. "How are you feeling?" He brushed a stray lock of hair off of her cheek.

She tried to give him a faint smile. The pain was choking her, mind numbing in its agony. Her legs felt blistered from the inside out. What had happened? Normally she felt painful twinges, but for her to feel such pain, something bad must have happened. All she remembered was Royce coming to her in the solar, and her being sleepy...

"You were poisoned, Leah." He straightened the blankets around her, tucking them under her chin and looking down at her with such concern that it made her heart clench. "Someone put something in that food that was brought to you in the solar. Do you remember who it was?"

Poisoned? What the hell? Someone had tried to kill her? She shook her head, remembering the man that had brought the basket of food to her. He was a servant, she'd guessed, but she hadn't recognized him. And what had he said? Something about how he'd been told to bring her the food. Silly her, she'd assumed it was Royce.

Apparently not. She struggled to sit up in bed, then fell back weakly. How long had she been out? How much time was left in the month?

His hand clasped over hers. "Calm down, Leah. You've been sick. Relax. Let me take care of you." His fingers tightened over her own. "First you take an arrow for me, now the poison," he said, his fingers rubbing her arm and stroking her skin, as if by touching her he'd reassure himself that she was fine. "Is there any trouble you've not gotten into yet, Leah?" The amused, relieved affection in his voice belied his unkind words.

She reached up to touch his cheek. She'd risk all kinds of things for him.

Pain awoke Leah the next day.

She regained consciousness with agony streaking through her limbs and cascading from her feet to her fingertips. The unnatural torment was all-encompassing, and Leah sat up in bed with one purpose in mind.

She had to get to the ocean.

Leah had tried to sneak out yesterday, but she was no more than three blindingly painful steps out the door when he'd found her, scolded her, and lovingly carried her back to her sickbed. She'd smiled at him, all the while biting her lip to keep from screaming at the anguish shooting through her limbs.

The thought of the task ahead of her was enough to make her stomach churn. It seemed such a long walk from Royce's chamber to hers, and then down the winding secret passage that led out, far away, to the beach. She stumbled out of the bed and nearly crashed onto the floor, the thick headboard the only thing keeping her upright. Black circled the edges of her vision as she took a tentative step. This wasn't going to work.

124

Yet... there was no other option. She had to get to the beach.

Grimly, she continued on. The passageway to her own small room seemed endless, but she made it. Kneeling over to touch the secret brick was almost enough to fell her, but she managed to struggle her way upright again and take the few shuffling steps. Luckily for her, she'd seen no servants on her way in, no one to stop her.

She hadn't taken more than a few steps down the dark passageway when she nearly tripped over a loose rock, stubbing her toe. A sobbing gasp of pain erupted from her mouth, and she bit her knuckles hard enough to taste blood. She was not any closer to the ocean now, and she'd spent at least a half-hour struggling to get this far. At the rate she was going, someone would discover she'd gone, and then Royce would think her a spy again. Or worse, they'd find out her secret.

A hand clasped her shoulder.

Startled, Leah turned, her eyes wide, straining to see in the darkness. No one would be here but herself... or maybe Muffin? But the hand on her shoulder was strong, and Leah's voice would not work.

"Leah," said Father Andrew, his cool voice bouncing off the walls of the narrow passageway around them. "I suspected I might find you here."

Gone was the thoughtful, soft thread of the priest's voice. In its place was a core of steel, an element of disdain that Leah had never heard before. She shifted her shoulder, and when she did, he dug his fingers into her skin even further.

"What do you do here?" He slid closer to her, his sweet, clean breath teasing the stagnant air about them. "Do you hide from Lord Royce? Searching for a lover?" When she remained silent, he chuckled. "I forgot. You cannot speak, or so you say. I suppose that is how you've kept your secret so long."

Ice flooded her veins, and Leah tensed. What did that mocking note in his voice mean? Why had he changed?

"Perhaps I have interrupted your nightly visit to the beach?" When she tried to jerk away from his hand, his fingers tightened painfully on her shoulder. "I wonder, does your lover know that you make these visits? That you can... talk? Among other things?"

He *knew*.

Father Andrew knew her secret. Fear shot through her, as fierce and painful as the feelings coursing through her legs. What would he do to her now? If he told Royce the truth, she'd fail at Muffin's game and her second chance would be gone.

"It is a shame, really," Father Andrew said, his voice soft as she tried to weakly jerk away again. "I thought you to be a good woman when I first met you. Perhaps a bit unlucky in your choice of profession, but still good. I came to check on you several times in your room, but you were always gone. Where did you go, I wonder? I had your room watched for a full night once, and you never came out, so I knew that you must have found another way out. Imagine my surprise when I followed you and your friend out here."

He'd seen Muffin. Oh God. Leah began to tremble.

"Your friend, is she a witch? Does she make a special deal with the devil? Have you sold your soul as well? Is that why he has cursed you with such a monstrous form? Half fish and half woman?"

Leah shook her head. Feebly, she tried to step away from him again, but he kicked her leg out from under her, and she fell to the ground in pain.

"Has it occurred to you, woman, that you are at my mercy? At God's mercy?" He leaned in close to her, his breath hissing close to her hair. "I tried to kill you with the poison, but it didn't work. Your witch's constitution is too strong for even the most potent of poisons, so I prayed

126

to God to help me deliver this castle from the bastard and his unholy minions." Hot spittle rained down on her face as he hissed above her. "And do you know what he told me?"

She shivered away from him, wanting to get away from his evil, cruel words.

The priest followed her, leaning in and grabbing her hair to force her face close to his. "He told me to use you."

Instead of letting her go, he slid a hand underneath her scorching, throbbing legs and lifted her up. At first Leah was too surprised to protest, but she ceased struggling when he began to carry her down the passageway, heading toward the beach. Her head lolled against his shoulder – she didn't understand his motives, but if it took her closer to her goal, so be it.

He said nothing to her for very long moments, not even when he turned sideways to slide out of the tunnel and began to cross the beach, though his legs dragged down in the sand with every step.

The surf was so close that the scent invaded her nostrils, and her mouth filled with saliva, her body so urgent for the release from pain that she could taste it. So close.

But the priest stopped mere feet from the water. "The Lord has told me to use you, Leah, and I will," he said, his voice soft. "You will be the tool that I will use to break Lord Royce, to turn him from this castle and return it to its rightful owner, Lord Rutledge."

She pushed at his arm in protest. She wanted in the water, but his fingers were digging into her thigh and he wouldn't let her go.

His eyes lit down on her, and behind the mask of kindness that reflected in their soft brown depths, there was a flicker of insanity. "You're going to help me bring down your precious Lord Royce, or I'm going to expose you for what you are."

Leah stilled in his arms, terror clenching her body. No!

The priest laughed at her terrified expression. "And that, my dear, is why you're going to help me." With a zealous grin, he dumped her into the water.

Chapter Fifteen

The relief that the ocean brought was a welcome one, and Leah's thoughts became clear for the first time in days. Clear enough that she recognized the hate blazing out of the priest's eyes as he watched her drag her tail up on the sand and wait to change back.

When she was done, she clutched the remnants of her sodden gown to her body and stared up at the priest. He stared down at her with an expressionless face, but his eyes could not hide his loathing. "A disgrace to God," he murmured, but helped her to her feet and brushed sand off her skirts. "Come," he said, his voice returning to the gentle tone it normally was. "We should return you to the keep before Lord Royce worries over you. That wouldn't do well for my plans at all."

Leah's brows furrowed together.

He patted her arm, as if launching back into his role as fatherly advisor. "I'll keep it simple for you. Any time that I approach and tell you that I'm to leave for my prayers and have my rosary in hand, you must do your part."

She stared up at him, uncomprehending.

He gave her a pitying, condescending smile. "Seduce him, of course. Keep Lord Royce distracted so I may go about robbing his coffers." He patted her on the back and released her. "I should think this would be easy enough for you, given your proclivities to share his bed already. Do not disappoint me."

Her fists clenched. She hated him.

He turned and walked away, heading down the beach in the opposite direction from her secret passage. "I must go. Remember what I have said and your life shall be preserved."

The chill in Leah's soul did not go away, even when she slipped back into Royce's bed.

Instead, she fell into an exhausted sleep. One without pain, one without physical strain, just sleep.

She slept for hours. Nightmares of the priest plagued her, and she bolted upright in the bed, chest heaving.

Next to her in the bed, a body shifted. "Leah?" Royce's husky whisper pierced the darkness and he touched her arm, stroking one hand up her smooth flesh. "Are you all right?"

She settled back in to bed next to him, still unsteady and shaking. The dream had seemed so real, and even lying in bed didn't soothe her nerves. She had to do something about Father Andrew. But what?

The backside of her body was suddenly pressed against yards of hot, male form, and she felt his face nuzzle into the back of her neck. "You smell like the sea, Leah," Royce mumbled against her hair. His arm tightened around her waist. "Go back to sleep."

She fell back into Royce's arms, but sleep was longer in coming.

The next few days, Leah was pleased to find, passed without incident. She was able to sneak out during the daylight hours when Royce was overseeing the daily duties of the castle, and her nights she spent cuddled

next to his side. He brought her easy things to eat –
soups, broths, mashes – and stroked her hair while she
slept. He stayed in the bedchamber with her for hours,
talking about his boyhood or asking her yes and no
questions about herself.

The only thing marring her happiness was the
priest's sinister demand. Leah thought and thought, but
no plan came to her that would work. If she didn't do
what he asked, he'd tell Royce her secret. Then she would
die and she still wouldn't be able to help Royce. So she
kept thinking, hoping desperately for inspiration.

One evening, Royce shooed away the chambermaids
after she'd eaten the nightly porridge that Maida insisted
upon. Curious at his actions, Leah tilted her head and
watched him from the bed, where she snuggled under the
covers.

"Did you want a bath this eve, Leah?"

Her eyes widened and she stilled in the bed, all ease
and laziness vanishing from her eyes. A bath would be a
very bad idea. To try and deflect him, she shook her head
and assumed her most pathetic expression, laying back
on the bed and half-closing her eyes out of exhaustion.
Royce took the hint and moved to her side. "If you're not
feeling well enough to share my bed in all ways, Leah, I
understand. But there's no need to hint at weakness. You
just tell me when you're ready." His eyes held a note of
amusement.

Leah blushed at the thought and smiled back at him.
He was a good man, for all his rough looks and hard
edges. She slid a hand out to him and smiled shyly.

He took it, linking his hand with hers and giving her
that hard-angled half-grin that made her knees melt.
"Mind if we play questions again?"

He was fascinated with her, that much was obvious.
And she could tell that her yes/no answers frustrated
him, but intrigued as well. When she nodded her

agreement, a wicked smile curved his mouth, sending her heart to fluttering. He leaned over her body and raked it with a long glance, hands reaching for the voluminous chemise. "In exchange for letting you loll about in bed, I'm going to give you a good rub-down. It'll make you feel better."

There was a downside to this?

He pulled the chemise over her head and stared down at her body. A low groan escaped his throat. "God's bones, Leah, but you've got a beautiful body." His hand slid across one thigh. "Long and lean everywhere, and curved in the right places."

She didn't have time to be embarrassed before he was flipping her over onto her stomach, his hands pinning her shoulders down on the bed before she could protest. "My rules, Leah. Let someone take care of you for a change."

Before she could protest further, his fingers were on her stiff, bare shoulders, kneading, and oh, it felt wonderful. She froze for a moment, and then melted against his hands. They were rough, and callused, and strong, and they knew just where to touch her. A small whimper of unexpected pleasure escaped her throat.

He chuckled at the sound of it, and she felt his hands sweep down the length of her back. "I suppose I should start asking before you fall asleep." His touch slid down her waist and settled on her buttocks. "Does this feel good?"

She grinned and raised one finger with a lazy motion, the symbol they'd come to use for 'yes'. Two fingers meant 'no'.

A pleased look came over his angular face, and his hands moved lower, massaging her buttocks. "You have a lovely bottom, Leah. So round and firm."

She wiggled it against his hands suggestively, feeling very languid and nice, indeed.

"Has anyone ever touched you like this before?" His voice had dropped to a lower note.

Leah lifted a second finger, indicating 'no'. She'd done her fair share of kissing, of course. But most of her dates had ended with some awkward fumbling and that was it, and she'd always been too busy with school to go after more. No one had ever touched her like Royce had, and he knew just where – and how – to make her body sing. Hot fingers slid up and down her flesh, kneading and working out the tension in her muscles, up and down her thighs and back up to her ass. She felt his thumb slide along the crease between her legs, sending skitters of excitement through her body. "Another question... have you ever been married?"

An easy enough one to answer, if she could concentrate on the question and not on what his fingers were doing. She waved the two fingers at him again.

"No man in your life except me? I find that hard to believe." He chuckled, and his fingers stroked between her legs again, just a brush of fingertips as he massaged her flesh, and Leah felt the soft whimper escape her throat once more. "What about your family? Are they still living?"

Not living was the same as not yet born, Leah supposed, so she raised the two fingers at him again and gave him a sensual smile.

He grunted assent. "Not really surprised by that. I don't know many men that would allow their well-bred daughters to become..." He stopped himself and she tensed under his hands, waiting for the inevitable shoe to drop. "The mistress to a bastard," he finally finished, his voice taking on a hard edge. "I can only think that Baron Rutledge must have seemed like a prime choice compared to me."

Leah turned over in the bed and sat up, looking up at him. The angles of his face were hard to read, but she detected a bit of self-loathing mixed in with the cynicism. He must have had a hard childhood, she thought. Unloved as a bastard, and then orphaned. Forgetting all about the gentle seduction he was playing on her body, she moved to his side and tilted her face toward his, waving her two fingers in the air for 'No'. Baron Rutledge would never be her choice.

He leaned down and gently kissed her mouth, the edges of his lips quirking up in a rueful smile. "Sometimes you're too good to be true, Leah." Royce's fingers brushed a long lock of hair away from the edge of her face.

She smiled up at him, but her smile faltered. Too good to be true was right.

She was a fraud.

"I want to give you something," he said, and left the bed, returning a moment later with a small velvet bag.

When he handed it to her, she was surprised at the weight of it. Leah gave him a surprised look, and when he gestured for her to open the bag, she did... and gasped at the sight. It was a jeweled belt. She pulled it out of the bag, staring at it in wonder. Golden rectangular links were hammered into small, flat links, each one adorned by a brilliant gemstone. The belt was long and linked at a circle in the waist, where it could lay flat against her pubic bone. It was lovely. It was expensive.

And looking at it, she knew she could never wear it around the keep. It was totally inappropriate for him to give her, and far richer than anything Ginny or the other castle women owned. It set her at a weird, uncomfortable place and flaunted her status. She clutched the links, torn between being touched by his thoughtfulness, and sad at the gift.

"Do you like it?"

What could she say? She leaned in and kissed him to show her thanks.

He wasn't there when she awoke the next morning.
Leah snuck down to the beach for a quick dip and was
back before the sun was high in the sky. Ginny helped
her dress, all smiles and chatter, and winked when Leah
blushed at her prying questions. "Lord Royce is down
visiting the blacksmith, Lady Leah, if you'd care to visit
him."

I must be really obvious, Leah thought to herself with
a rueful smile, and nodded at Ginny.

It took a little time to find her way outside. She didn't
know what the blacksmith's foundry looked like, Leah
realized, squinting at the bright afternoon sunlight. She
only paused for a short time—the day was too lovely to
spend upstairs. Her legs felt good, her body felt good, and
she hadn't seen the priest in the past few days. She
gathered her skirts and began to walk the bailey, a smile
on her face and her steps light.

A hut on the far end of the castle courtyard proved to
be the smith's domain. She could smell the scent of metal
and smoke from a good distance away, and her steps
gravitated toward that. A group of men stood outside,
near a rather large horse. She noticed a familiar face
holding the bridle – Christophe – and he had his hand on
the large black beast's muzzle.

He scowled in greeting at the sight of her. Well, she
supposed, not everyone was going to love her. She wasn't
interested in his scowl, though, but in Royce's broad
shoulders and mussed hair – and damn fine legs – as he
talked to the heavily muscled, squat man that was surely
the blacksmith.

Perhaps this wasn't a good time for her to interrupt.
Hesitant, Leah hung back, clasping her hands and

waiting patiently for Royce to finish. She studied him as she waited.

He listened to the smith complain, just nodded and asked questions. Royce leaned in and spoke to the blacksmith, putting his hand on the man's shoulder. She leaned in as well, straining to hear what he said.

"Greetings, Leah."

She froze at the sound of that voice. Once, she thought it was gentle and loving, but now the tone seemed overly sweet and unnatural. Leah turned slowly and offered a faint smile to Father Andrew in greeting, her hands fisting in her skirts.

He gave her a soft smile and moved to stand next to her. "Enjoying the weather? It's a fine morning." When she continued to stare at him, he tilted his head and regarded her. "Feeling better? You look much improved from when I saw you last."

Leah pasted on a wan smile. She gave him a quick nod, and then turned her attention back to Royce. Her skin prickled when she realized that Christophe was still watching her.

Royce had finished with the blacksmith and turned to her, the edges of a sensual smile on his face. The warmth in his eyes as he looked down at her was apparent. "Good afternoon, Father, Leah," he said, his greeting for both of them, but the steamy look in his eyes was purely for her. He came to her side and took her hand in his. "What are you doing out of bed? Feeling better?"

Christophe's narrowed eyes were still focused in on her, and his gaze darted to the priest. She forced a brilliant smile to her face and nodded eagerly at Royce, looking up into his eyes. She felt like a huge fraud.

"Is there a problem with the blacksmith, my lord?" Father Andrew's soft, inquiring tones grated on Leah's nerves. "He looks to be most distraught."

Her gaze went back to the short, heavily muscled man as he disappeared back into the forge.

"Nothing that would concern you, Father." Royce tucked Leah's hand into the crook of his arm and placed his own over it, a possessive, endearing gesture that warmed her heart. "There was a problem with the quality of some of the metal that was purchased prior to my retaking of the castle."

"Indeed." Father Andrew sounded ashamed. "I'm sorry to say that Baron Rutledge did not think highly of Gideon's works in relation to the forge. He focused more on other things."

The look on Royce's face was dismissive, and he gave the priest a curt nod when the old Baron's name was brought up. "Yes, well, King Henry gave me leave to retake the castle, and I plan to fix a good many things now that it is mine again. I've given Gideon the funds – and the permission – to do the best work he sees fit, so you need not concern yourself with the matter." He began to walk away from the forge, Leah tucked firmly at his side as he started across the courtyard.

Father Andrew followed them, still all smiles. "That is good news indeed, Lord Royce. You will forgive me if I seem a bit prying. I am merely concerned for the well-being of one of my flock, and Gideon has been unhappy for some time." Cheer wreathed his face. "It is good to know that you are taking such good care of the people here."

Leah wanted to punch him in his fake mouth.

Royce glanced down at her, as if seeing the annoyance she fought so hard to hide flashing across her face. He stopped, his hands sliding around her waist. "Would you excuse us, Father Andrew? I need to speak to Leah privately."

The priest appeared surprised by the request, but the soft smile returned, curving his lips once more. "Of course, my lord. Forgive me for disturbing you. I must be off to pray." He raised his hand, showing his rosary to the two of them. "Good day to you, Lord Royce, Leah."

The rosary in his hand stilled Leah. He hadn't forgotten his ultimatum to her, and as she watched him walk across the courtyard in his long, dark robes, she resisted the urge to cry.

Warm, gentle hands squeezed her waist, reminding her of the present. "Is something bothering you, Leah?"

She looked up into Royce's concerned face. Father Andrew's insidious words rang through her mind. *"Seduce him. Keep him distracted so I may go about robbing his coffers."*

What could she do? Father Andrew would tell her secret if she didn't do what he asked. Even though she hated herself for doing so, Leah took Royce's hand in hers and brushed her mouth against his knuckles, giving him a suggestive look and letting her teeth graze against the sensitive flesh. An unhappy twinge shot through her, but she pushed the feeling aside.

Royce's eyes darkened, and concern was replaced with the hot stroke of desire. He pulled her closer to him, the front of her hips brushing against his, and she felt the evidence of his desire. "Are you... recovered, then, lady? Enough for the eager attentions of a bastard warlord?"

Excitement rushed through her, and she forced herself to remain slow and sensual as she flipped his palm over and gently bit the flesh there.

He groaned and slid a hand under her knees, hoisting her into his arms as if she weighed nothing. Surprised, Leah hid her face, blushing. She could feel the hot stares of everyone in the keep as they watched their lord carry his leman across the castle grounds.

Royce chuckled. "Don't be such a coward, Leah. If you play a seduction game, don't be surprised when it works."

He leaned in and whispered against her hair. "And they're smiling – the men are envious that I get to make love to you, and the women are jealous because of the attention I show you. You worry too much as to what others think – I am the master of this castle, and I shall do as I please."

Oh, really? That sounded like a challenge if she'd ever heard one. Leah unburied her face and quirked an eyebrow at him. Her hand slid between the laces that stole up the yoke of his tunic, and she maneuvered her hand inside, brushing her fingers against one of his nipples suggestively.

He groaned against her hair. "Someplace private. We need someplace private right now or I'm going to take you in the middle of this courtyard."

They passed by another horse in front of a low building, and Leah pointed at it, feeling rather bold at his encouraging responses.

"The stables? You're a wicked woman," he murmured against her hair.

The stables? Oh lord, that wasn't quite where she'd imagined having their romantic interlude, but she noticed that he didn't complain. In fact, he changed course and made a beeline for the building, shoving the heavy wooden doors open and startling the stable boys inside.

"Everyone out," he growled, and the boys nodded and touched their forelocks before racing out the door.

Leah began to rethink the whole thing when the door slammed shut behind them, leaving only trickles of light streaming in between the wooden boards and the thatched roof. He set her down gently on her feet.

And then Royce's hot, hungry mouth was on hers and she forgot about whether or not this was a good idea. She returned his kisses with an intensity of her own, and her arms went around him, her nails digging through the back of his tunic. His hands slid down her waist and grasped her buttocks, kneading them and sliding her hips against his groin. A familiar whimper escaped her.

"Ah, Leah," he groaned against her lips, his fingers digging into the flesh of her behind. "It's been too many days since I've tasted that sweet flesh of yours. It's been torturing me for days... you're in my dreams when I sleep, teasing me with your eyes and those long legs of yours."

Her hands slid over his back, seeking purchase, but the thick weave of his tunic kept her from finding what she wanted, and she gave a little groan of frustration, her hands drifting down and searching for the edge of his tunic, jerking it up and through his belt and sliding her hands around the smooth skin of his back. The hard muscles played under her hands, and she gave a sigh of pure delight at the touch.

She felt his hand searching under her skirts, even as she reached down toward the front of his hose to unfasten them.

He growled in frustration at the layers of skirts preventing him from finding her. "You wear too many clothes, Leah," he said, his mouth moving against her neck and nipping gently. She gasped at the sensation, her hands flexing on his back in surprised pleasure.

Suddenly she was being lifted off the ground, and her hands dug into his skin for purchase, clinging to his waist. He grabbed her by the buttocks and hauled her a few staggering steps, her hips cradled against his erection, lips sucking at her neck with the same fevered intensity she felt. The wall slammed up against her back, surprising her and nearly knocking the wind out of her, but she forgot all about it when his mouth returned to hers and his tongue thrust at the same time his hips did. She wrapped her legs around his waist, letting him support her against the wall.

"Put your arms around my neck," he instructed, his hands digging through her skirts again, and she did, sliding them over his shoulders and biting at his lower lip, teasing it gently with her teeth.

And then she felt his hand find her bare legs, and she moaned her encouragement as her skirts were shoved to the side, her hips now naked and cradled against his breeches. His fingers slid between their pinned hips, sliding against her folds. "You're so hot and ready for me, Leah. God, you're wet." He shifted her against the wall and she clung to him, and then she felt his erection slide up against the hot slickness of her sex, searching, and then he thrust home, pinning her against the wall.

She inhaled sharply at the shock of him, feeling that mix of pain and pleasure shoot through her again as her body stretched to accommodate him. The pain vanished within moments, and when he thrust again, there was nothing but the stroke of pure pleasure. The angle of his body against hers rubbed her clit with every stroke, doubling the intensity of each slow grind.

"Leah," he moaned against her mouth. "Ah, Leah. Your body is so sweet." His hands held her hips in a death grip.

Her hands clutched at him frantically, her legs wrapped around his waist as her body bore down against his with each thrust, encouraging him every step of the way. The wall against her was uncomfortable, but the thought only registered briefly in her mind, chased away with each achingly sweet thrust into her body.

And then he was whispering against her mouth again, and one of his hands slid away from her hips and latched on to her nipple through the fabric of the dress. "Come for me," he whispered, stroking the sensitive nub through the thick fabric. "I want to hear you come, Leah. I want to hear you gasp with pleasure... as I thrust into you... and I want to feel you clench around me... as you lose control." With each pause, his lips met hers, seeking, teasing.

With a few quick strokes of his fingers, she shattered against him, crying out as her body quaked with shudders and she came.

"That's it, Leah," he murmured against her, clutching her body to his as he thrust again. "Come for me, sweetling." His thrusts became more insistent, and the words on his lips died into a low growl as he continued to thrust, harder and harder, as she moaned and her body continued to shudder. The orgasm had barely stopped before she felt her body tensing, anticipating the next.

A loud groan was ripped from his throat as his body shuddered and he came inside her as well, one final hard thrust sending her floating amidst the shockwaves again.

It took a few minutes for Leah's racing heart to return to normal, and when it did she ran a hand through his sweaty, tangled locks of hair. His head rested on her shoulder, and he still had her propped up against the wall – a wall that was in danger of giving her some very nasty splinters.

He turned his face in and she felt his breath against her neck. "You make me mad with wanting you, Leah," Royce said, a chuckle in his throat. "My men are going to be giving me odd looks for days."

She was glad it was dark so he couldn't see the blush on her face, and instead just tapped on his shoulder, indicating that she wanted to get up.

He let her go gently, and their bodies slid apart, Leah's legs rubbery and sweat dampening the hair of her brow. She heard him lacing his breeches again in the dark, then felt his hands on her skirt, helping her smooth it. Her hand found his and she leaned in, bringing her lips to his for a long, meaningful kiss that promised many things. His breath became ragged again. "We can go upstairs..." he suggested, and she squeezed his hand in agreement. Upstairs sounded very nice, indeed.

"Fire!" Someone shouted, and then everything was forgotten.

Royce muttered an expletive and jerked away from Leah, running for the stable doors. The door flung open a moment later and sunlight flooded into the room. Leah trailed after him, trying to straighten her skirts and stumbling along.

Dread made her steps slow as she looked for the telltale smoke and found it over the blacksmith's small hut. Oh no. She watched, the world streaming by in slow motion as commoners rushed past, buckets of water in hand, hurrying to the smithy. The crowd of people near it was in motion at all times, moving and swaying as people brought water and then ran away again. Standing in the middle of the throng was Royce, shouting orders and handing buckets.

This was her fault.

She stood back, her arms wrapped around herself, unable to do more as they worked to put out the fire. Even when the flames died out and there was nothing left but charred and sooty rubble, she couldn't force herself to go forward. She felt responsible.

The sight of Father Andrew stirred her into action. As she watched, he approached one of the men who lay on the ground and lifted his head, a look of concern on his soft features. Leah found herself rushing over, a curious mix of dread and reluctance mixing through her as she approached.

Royce moved to the priest's side as well, maneuvering there at the same time that she did. The blacksmith lay on the ground, his eyes closed and his mouth slack, and she bit her knuckle. Had Father Andrew killed the man?

Royce rubbed his forehead, leaving a dark smear of soot across his face. "How is he, Father?"

"Knocked unconscious."

Leah nearly fainted with relief. Thank god.

The priest spoke again. "And the foundry? Can it be saved?"

Royce's response was less than cheering. "The roof collapsed early. I doubt there's much that can be saved in there." He sounded tired – tired and depressed. Leah stood, going to his side and putting a hand on his chest in concern.

He gave her a tired smile and a kiss on her forehead. "Go back to my chambers, Leah. There's a lot of work to be done here, and you're still too weak to be up and about all day."

She shook her head.

"Please, Leah, for me. I won't be able to help the men while I'm thinking about you all the time. Understand?"

Leah nodded and touched his hand, heading back toward the castle. She wanted to look back at the priest again, but she didn't dare. Royce had mentioned money earlier in the day, and she had no doubt that whatever was in the smithy was gone now. As she headed back down the great hall, she saw Christophe again, heading through with some rope and a few other men, and the look he shot her was accusing.

She deserved it.

Chapter Sixteen

She woke up later that night as Royce put his arms around her, pulling her close to him. He smelled like smoke and sweat, a strong, pungent combination that filled her nostrils. He seemed so weary and sad, though, that she didn't have the heart to push him away. Instead, she turned to him and stroked his hair away from his face, wishing she had words to offer him comfort.

"The money's gone. The forge was robbed, and no doubt whoever stole the money set the fire. The coins have disappeared, as well as the jewels and gold I had set aside as a gift for the king." He buried his face against the soft swell of her breasts.

Leah slipped out of his arms and went to her small trunk. She pulled out the velvet bag with the beautiful golden belt and handed it to him.

"No," he said harshly. "That's yours. I won't strip gifts from you simply to have them snatched by another thief."

She nodded and replaced the bag back in the trunk, then slid back into bed with him. Just thinking about the belt made her feel guilty, but of course she couldn't tell him that. She couldn't say anything.

He pulled her close. "Someone's working against me, Leah, and unless I find out who it is, they're going to drive me out of this castle. I won't be able to afford my men, and I'll be forced to sell my sword to whoever will

145

have me." His arms tightened around her. "I'll be a landless bastard again, Leah. A man unable to keep his own castle without it falling about his ears."

Her hands soothed his brow, smoothed his hair, and she closed her eyes so he wouldn't see the frustrated tears that threatened to well from her eyes. It was her fault. All she had to do was somehow tell him who was really behind the deeds, and he'd be free. He'd have his castle.

And she'd have nothing. No Royce, no second chance at life. Nothing. She hesitated a moment, then touched his chest, trying to get his attention.

"What is it?"

Leah gestured, trying to explain to him. That it was the priest. That he was stealing money from Royce under his nose. That she knew exactly what was going on. But the more she gestured, the more Royce simply looked confused. Frustrated, Leah clenched her hands into fists.

He kissed her forehead. "You can tell me in the morning."

If only she could.

"Pack your dresses, Leah," Royce said to her one morning a week later. "We leave at noon."

She propped up on one elbow and watched him with bleary eyes, shoving her hair out of her face. Pack? What was he talking about?

Royce was across the room, dressing in a worn pair of breeches. His back faced her, and for a moment she admired the long, muscular line of his shoulders. In the last week, they'd gotten to know each other rather intimately, and there wasn't an inch of skin on him that she hadn't kissed. Now, instead of blushing when he turned and gave her a lascivious, teasing look, she returned it with a smile.

The last week had been one of the most enjoyable – and most frustrating - of her life. Over and over, she'd tried to tell Royce what was going on. She had to be careful; if Father Andrew found out she was attempting to rat him out, he'd tell her secret. She needed to somehow tell Royce the truth without alerting the priest. But no matter how much she gestured and signaled, no one was able to understand her. She'd have tried to write out the answer, but had no paper. She didn't know what to do.

So she hid in Royce's suite of rooms the entire week. She'd managed to avoid Father Andrew as well, switching up the times of her beach visits and supplementing her needs with the occasional private bath or two. The rest of the time she'd spent with Royce, learning about each other, making love, or just enjoying the other's quiet company.

Leah had fallen head over heels in love with him. She had denied it even to herself for the first few days, but as time passed, it became more obvious. Her heart pounded when he entered the room. A smile from him would make her day – and a frown could easily break it. She lived for the moments when she was with him, utterly aware how time was ticking away.

Muffin had disappeared after scolding Leah and hadn't reappeared. Leah wondered about this, and it was always at the back of her mind, niggling like a toothache. It bothered her, but not enough to ruin her happiness.

Royce tossed a tunic at her head, laughing when she sputtered and sat upright in the massive bed. "I can see I've taught my wench to be lazy." He leaned in for a quick kiss once her face was revealed again and took the tunic from her, shrugging it over his head. "King Henry is visiting a nearby holding and he's promising a tourney. Last I saw the king, I vowed I'd go and joust for him."

Uneasy, Leah slid off the bed and moved to Royce's side, lacing the front of his tunic. She shook her head at him, trying to convey that she didn't want him to go.

He didn't seem to notice her reluctance. "I promised the king I'd be there several months back, when he approved my taking back of the castle. However, I didn't foresee the problems that we've been having lately." A dark frown tightened the edges of his mouth. "Still, a promise to the king is not one you can break. Which is why you're going with me."

Surprised at that, Leah pulled back, unease shooting through her. There were too many factors to consider. What if something happened to the castle while they were gone? What if Father Andrew robbed him blind? Worse, what if Royce took her with him and there was no place for her to ease her legs?

"Not to worry, Leah. Lots of men bring their mistresses to things such as this. It's not as if anyone will bother you." He touched her cheek and brought her face to his for a possessive kiss. "Besides, I'll be gone for near on a fortnight, and that makes for a long time to have a cold bed."

She couldn't put words to her fears. The look on his face told her enough; it was a done deal. She wanted to go with him, even if it was impossible with her legs. If she could keep him away from Father Andrew, she'd have the time to tell him what was going on. She didn't know how long a fortnight was, but if it was longer than the week and a half she had left, she'd have to think of something.

And fast.

The weather was clear and cold when they left Northcliffe, a stiff breeze blowing through Leah's thick clothing and making her shudder. She huddled closer to Royce's back from her perch behind him on his horse, and tried not to think about how high up they were, or how uncomfortable riding like this actually was.

Royce waved one last goodbye at Christophe and Giles. He'd left them in charge, and that made Leah feel moderately better. Out of all of them, she trusted those two to keep Royce's possessions safe.

The priest had insisted on coming with them. "I've an old friend that lives there," he'd said with a soft, almost-genuine smile. "I'd love to see him again if you don't mind one old priest traveling with you."

From the wrinkle in Royce's brow, he'd been frustrated by the request, but he was too polite and respectful of the priest to disagree. He'd had a mule saddled for Father Andrew, and he paced along behind them. The ride, for the most part, was long, uncomfortable, and insignificant. The soldiers traded jokes back and forth as they traveled, and even Leah found herself smiling and blushing at a particularly coarse verse or two.

When the sun went down, their small group began to set up camp. Royce helped Leah slide down the side of the horse, her legs boneless and shooting with pain. In addition to the muscle soreness from being unused to horseback riding, she had her mermaid aches, as well. He chuckled when she nearly collapsed in his arms and held her steady. "Go sit down on, Leah. I'll come and get you when our tent is ready." He gave her a lascivious wiggle of his eyebrows and smacked her on the rump, no doubt enjoying the squeal of surprise that she emitted.

Leah hobbled over to a fallen log in a copse a short distance away, trying not to think about the tingling pain shooting through her limbs. She rubbed her legs as she waited, hoping that she'd be able to swing something to help the pain. A sponge bath? That probably wouldn't work. Maybe a nearby pond? It'd be scummy, judging from the vegetation around here, but a dip was a dip, and it would help her legs—

"Mind if I sit down with you, my dear?"

She looked up reluctantly, and Father Andrew smiled down at her. Her eyes went to Royce. He was standing with his men, discussing something intent, his back turned to her. She glanced at the priest and shrugged, trying to seem casual though her heart was hammering in her breast.

"You were limping," he noted. "Is it your beast-legs? Do they crave the water?"

Her eyes widened, shocked that he would admit something so loudly, but the others didn't seem to notice. To quiet him, she glared and gave him a curt nod, turning away and clenching her hands so as not to rub her legs any more. If only she could get rid of him.

"How are you enjoying your trip?" He cocked his head, examining her as if he would a strange bird. When she responded with a 'so-so' wiggle of her hand that he didn't seem to understand, the smile on his face grew larger. "Why do you continue to pretend, Leah? Why won't you speak? Royce won't hear you, and we both know that you can talk."

She glared at him, her nervous hands smoothing her skirts. They were crumpled into a web of wrinkles after the long ride, and she didn't have many dresses. Besides, it gave her something to focus on other than the priest's too-nosy eyes.

"Do you know who will be at this tourney, Leah?" The priest leaned back on the log, stretching and relaxing as if he had not a care in the world. "A great many important men, I imagine. Men that hate your lover, and men like the king that cannot see his flaws no matter

150

how they pointed out." He chuckled to himself, as if enjoying a private joke. "I mean to bring those flaws into the light a bit more."

She glared at him, hating that he held her fate in his hand.

"You see, the king told Royce that he owed a tithe – and a rather hefty one – if he retook Northcliffe from Baron Rutledge. And I have it on very good authority that Royce keeps this tithe on him at all times, though I imagine he'll divest himself of it when you and him…" He blushed. "You know. The point is, when he is sleeping, you can take the tithe from him. I need you to steal it."

Steal it? Get Royce in trouble with the king? Frowning fiercely, Leah shook her head and moved to stand up, but the priest put a staying hand on her arm.

"I need you to get this for me… and it'll be the last thing you'll have to do. Trust me."

Trust him? She'd sooner trust the devil. She jerked her arm away and scowled down at him.

The priest stood. His delicate fingers brushed flakes of tree-bark off of his robes. "Just do as I ask, Leah. I'd hate to see you get hurt." Her eyes narrowed at his words, but he continued blithely on. "Imagine the pain Royce would feel to see your… true nature."

The blood drained from her face.

Father Andrew smiled, tucking his hands into his long sleeves. "I see that you'll do as I ask, then? I assure you that he will never find out the truth as long as you behave." He chuckled, a humorless little laugh. "After all, it's not as if you'll tell him, right?"

She flinched.

The priest reached out to pat her on the shoulder. "My apologies, my dear. That was cruel of me. I shall pray to God for forgiveness for my petty sins." He gestured at a copse of trees in the darkening distance. "If you're looking for water, there's a stream a short walk up the road."

He left her after that, a small, pleased smile playing on his lips. She sat back down on the log, trembling, and she wasn't able to stop shaking until long after Royce came to fetch her.

Royce mistook her trembling for fatigue, scooping her in his arms and taking her back to their tent. She tucked her head against his shoulder and let him carry her in. Inside the tent there was a makeshift bed that didn't seem to be more than a pile of blankets, and a few bags for their things. The interior was cold and dark.

Crossing to the bed, Royce gently laid her down amid the blankets. "Rest, Leah. You're exhausted. Get some sleep. Tomorrow we should arrive at the tourney."

A surge of possession shot through her, and Leah sat up in bed. She didn't want him to leave. Her hand stole to his body, and she grabbed him by the hem of his tunic, tugging him down.

"Leah?" The question rumbled in his throat, and she knew it was too dark to make out her face, so he bent down. "What's bothering you?"

Her hands stole up his body and she searched for his face in the darkness. Leah's lips found his and she kissed him possessively. She wanted to be inside his skin at this moment, to have him possess her and make her forget everything that was going wrong right now. She needed him.

She felt Royce stiffen in surprise, before he clenched his arms around her and slid down to the bed, taking her with him. Her frantic hands slid along the front of his braies and felt the erection that strained there, hot and hard, and she felt a surge of satisfaction. "Leah," he groaned against her mouth. "Are you sure...? My men are just outside..."

Her hand slid inside his hose and that was the last time he talked for quite some time.

When she awoke again later that night, the voices outside had gone quiet. Leah lay in bed for a long moment, her eyes open and body tense as she listened for sounds. Next to her, Royce slept, his breathing deep and even. Experimentally, she wiggled a toe under the blankets. Pain crashed through her lower legs, like ripples on a pond, spreading out from the movement.

There was no way she could avoid finding the stream. Not if she hoped to be able to ride behind Royce tomorrow without crying in agony the whole time. Leah held her breath and slowly eased out from under the blankets, every nerve ending tense as she waited for Royce to wake. She'd just explain that she was going to the bathroom, or something along those lines. It was a plausible excuse, she told herself, even if her heart hammered in her breast at the thought of being caught.

But she didn't have to worry. Royce continued to sleep, his breath low and even, his body unmoving. Relieved, Leah got to her feet and pulled on her chemise, unknotting the tent flap and peeking outside. No one was awake – the huddled shapes near the banked fire were all unmoving. She tiptoed out, holding her breath with each new step.

She managed to walk through the camp without waking a soul. Her eyes squinted as she stared into the dark, trying to determine the direction that Father Andrew had mentioned the stream would be. She'd forgotten her shoes, but it was such a fragile annoyance in comparison to the true pain that shot through her limbs with every step. Still, it'd make the going slow.

With the darkness, she misjudged the path and stumbled through one particularly bushy set of undergrowth, tumbling into the stream from above. Her ankle gave a sharp crack and pain shot through her leg, and her chin slammed into the bank. Well, she'd found the stream. As her legs began to transform, she jerked the chemise over her head and tossed it onto the shore, letting her body sink under the water, her muscles relaxing.

When she surfaced again, Muffin was there, her legs swinging on the edge of the riverbank, and smiling down at her. She was dressed in a toga, her feet clad in golden, ropy-looking sandals, and a wreath of leaves propped up on her brow. "Hello, my girl. How are things going with that handsome man?"

Pleased at the sight of the fairy godmother, Leah sat upright in the water and propped her arms up on the shelf of soft dirt next to where Muffin sat. "Where have you been? I've been worried that you forgot all about me."

Muffin patted her hand. "Not to worry, my dear. I'm a busy woman, but I'd never forget you. There were other girls to be seen to, and I'm afraid I got a bit carried away."

"Other girls like me?"

"You're the only mermaid at the moment," she said, "but in similar situations, yes." Muffin smiled down at Leah. "Why don't you tell me how it's going?"

A knot formed in Leah's throat, and she had to struggle to speak around it. "It's awful."

"Oh dear." Muffin's lined face pursed in sympathy. "That terribly?"

Bit by bit, the story of Father Andrew and his manipulations came spilling out. She told Muffin everything that had happened, up to this evening with his request for her to steal the tithe and break Lord Royce from the king's favor once and for all. The moon grew high in the skies and Leah began to shiver from the cold stream as she spoke, but she still continued to pour her heart out to Muffin. The fairy godmother never interrupted, just listened and clucked at the appropriate parts.

"I just don't know what to do," Leah said at one point, wiping at the tears on her face.

"There, there, dear," Muffin said, stroking the top of Leah's wet head. "Come out of the water and get dressed, and we'll discuss it."

Leah did as she was bid, pulling herself out of the stream and waiting for her tail to transform. Once it did, she slipped into the billowy chemise, the hem now torn and muddy. She felt like a child as she sat in the grass next to Muffin and tucked her legs under her, hands fussing with the wet, tangled strands of hair that covered her shoulders. "If you were in my position, Muffin, what would you do?"

"You mean, choose between saving your hide or his? I can't decide that for you. That's what you're here to do."

Leah frowned at her.

Royce realized that Leah was missing when he reached for her warm body and found nothing but empty bed beside him. He cracked an eye open, peering in the darkness for her form. When he didn't see her, he dressed and left the tent, scanning the rest of the campsite. Where could she have gone?

The night watchman gave him a curious look, but Royce waved him off. He'd noticed that she'd kept staring off into the distance, into the thick copse a short ways away that had a running stream through it. Did she know the villagers the next field over? Irritated that she'd gone and left in the middle of the night without warning, Royce headed in that direction. What could have possessed the woman – who normally seemed sane and level-headed for all her odd silence – to trek off after dark by herself? He refused to allow worry to creep into his mind. There were a dozen terrible things that could happen to a lone woman traveling after dark. He wouldn't think about that. Hell, he cared for the wench – cared for her more than he'd cared for anything in a long time, and the thought of her falling prey to highway brigands drew a cold slice through his gut.

He strode through the dark, hand on the pommel of his sword in readiness. A small stream came into view some minutes later and he stopped at its banks, wondering if Leah had even come this way. He was chasing nothing more than a ghost in the darkness. Disheartened, he turned away from the stream and glanced around.

A light, feminine sigh drifted by on the wind and he froze in place, muscles tensing.

"Muffin," the voice said, and the sound was sweet and soft, and just a touch melancholy. "I don't know what to do. Royce trusts me, and if I do this, I'll lose that trust forever."

It felt as if ice-water poured through his veins. Slowly, Royce turned back to the stream. The soft, feminine voice was coming just from down the stream a bit, and he stole back into the shadows of the nearby trees, careful to approach soundlessly. His fingers gripped his sword pommel with intensity, and he brushed aside the leaves, dreading what he would see there.

Leah sat on the riverbank nearby, hugging her knees to her chest, her hair wet, as she talked to another figure that he couldn't see.

Talked.

The lying, deceiving bitch could talk the whole time.

Rage shuddered through him, and he resisted the overwhelming urge to crash through the underbrush and grab her by the arms and shake her, shake her until the answers he wanted spilled out. *Why? Why would she lie to him?*

Instead, he gritted his teeth and forced himself to listen to her low, gentle voice as each deceitful word dripped out of those beautiful lips.

"He's going to find out, Muffin." Leah laid her cheek on her knee, her pale face gleaming wetly in the moonlight. She'd been crying. "And when he finds out, he's not going to love me anymore."

"Does he love you now?" The other voice asked.

"Not yet," Leah said. "But... I love him." Her words ended in a broken half-sob. "I never thought this would be so hard. What am I going to do if I can't make him love me? I have to. It's what I came here to do."

So, the lying little wench had come here intent on seducing him? And now that her plan was failing, she was crying her eyes out to another? Disgust curled through Royce's stomach, and he vowed that he'd never give her the satisfaction of hearing him admit his feelings. All tender feeling for her had vanished once she'd opened that sweet, lying mouth of hers.

"Well, I must go," the other voice said, perking his attention. "I've a certain someone to meet up with, and he doesn't like to be kept waiting."

Baron Rutledge, he thought immediately. Pretty Leah was nothing more than a spy sent by his worst enemy to get him to let his guard down. Worst of all, he'd fallen for it. No doubt she was behind the string of unlucky happenings at the castle. He thought of Lady Matilda's outraged claims, of her showing the money found in Leah's sewing basket. He'd assumed it was the ranting of a jealous woman intent on destroying her rival. But now the pieces fell into place with a clarity that was startling and disheartening.

On the shore, Leah nodded her understanding to her companion, but made no move to get up. "I'll head back to camp in a minute. I need to compose myself. I'll wake Royce for sure if he hears me crying."

Too late for that, Royce thought, the irony slashing into his soul. He felt cold inside, numb. Leah had shown her true colors and completely blindsided him. He melted back into the shadows and headed back to camp, his heart hardened against the soft weeping in the distance.

He would not fall prey to her wiles again.

Royce was treating her oddly, Leah decided the next morning. It was nothing she could put her finger on, but the coolness was there just the same. He wouldn't look at her when she dressed – quite the change from the affectionate morning caresses she normally woke up to. When she gave him a concerned look and touched his arm, he shrugged her away and stepped aside to buckle his sword. "Just thinking about the day, Leah. Don't pay attention to me."

How could she not?

Frustrated, Leah finished dressing on her own – no mean task given that her dress laced up on the sides, which made it difficult to reach. She braided her hair like everything was normal, and ate the breakfast that one of the soldiers provided to her, all the while her mind racing. Had Royce noticed her leaving the tent last night? Had he overheard her conversation with Father Andrew?

Surely not... she was still here and still cursed to be a mermaid.

It was a long ride that day, made worse by muscles stiff from the day before and Royce's silence. When she put her arms around him, she could have sworn that he stiffened, and she had to blink back tears. *But I love you,* she wanted to whisper against his skin.

But of course, she could say nothing, only stew in miserable silence. She thought of the too-short time that she had left. Less than a week. She'd failed in her goal; Royce didn't love her – right now he could barely tolerate her. She didn't know why.

The calm murmur of the guardsmen escalated a few hours later, when Leah was weary and slumped against Royce's back. She sat up when a half-cheer erupted from the men and the talk became livelier. With her arms encircling Royce's waist, she could feel him tense as he caught sight of whatever the men did, and Leah sat upright, straining to catch a glimpse over Royce's broad shoulders.

Her eyes could barely make out the flutter of a colorful banner in the distance. The flash of red caught her eye, then disappeared as Royce turned his head. "Leah," he said, his voice a low growl. "Stay still."

They must be at the tourney. Soon, they'd see the king, and soon she'd have to steal from Royce and ruin his life. Her last week with him was to be spent in misery, watching him as his life was destroyed when the tithe was stolen and Northcliffe taken from him.

She couldn't do it.

She might want to save herself, but not as his expense. Leah began to turn over a rebellious plan in her mind. If she could see the tithe before-hand, perhaps she could pass off an imposter tithe to the priest.

And then maybe she'd be able to leave this interlude with her scruples intact, if not her heart.

Chapter Seventeen

Leah peeked outside the small tent and stared at the goings-on around her with a mixture of longing and fear.

The tourney was a huge muddle of people – loud, shouting, boisterous, and all excited to be there. A sea of tents nestled in the grassy meadows at the base of an imposing castle perched atop a nearby hill.

As soon as they'd arrived the men had begun to set up camp, erecting new, colorful tents embossed with Royce's colors and made of fine, elegant materials. Leah remembered that someone had told her that Royce had made his fortune doing tourneys. That would explain the ease and delight that shone on the men's faces as they prepared the camp. Royce's tent was the largest one, meant to be both receiving area and living quarters, and was a far cry from their small traveling tent. These were festive, expensive encampments that spoke volumes of the prestige and wealth of the owner.

Their camp was set up in the midst of everything, much to Leah's dismay. Royce had disappeared not long after they'd arrived, leaving Leah to linger about the camp, feeling uncomfortable and unwanted as she watched his men erect the last of the tents. They'd ignored her.

She spent her time peeking out of the tent and watching the crowd. The men outnumbered the women two to one. The few women that she'd seen strolling the grounds were always accompanied and they dressed in gowns that would have put Lady Matilda's finery to shame. Anyone that saw Leah would immediately guess that she had no status, thanks to her lack of adornment. Royce was doing himself no favors by bringing her with him, Leah realized. She wasn't going to help amend the status of his low birth with her presence.

The sun went down and Royce did not return, and the revelry outside of the tent continued. Leah's nerves frayed more with every passing second. With a throng such as this, she'd never be able to steal away to ease her aching legs. She was well and truly trapped in the tent. Despairing, Leah fell into an exhausted slumber.

She woke the next morning, disoriented. Birds were singing, and the grounds were strangely quiet for a change. Unease prickled through her skin, until she heard the low roar of a crowd in the distance. The jousting games must have started. Royce hadn't returned to her last night. She stared at the empty tent around her, wondering if she'd be left alone until the tourney was over.

She lay back in the bed and drifted back into a lazy, depressed slumber. When her eyes drifted open again, she gasped at the sight of Royce standing over her, a hard look on his face. There were dark circles under his eyes, as if he hadn't slept. "Get dressed."

Leah sat up in the bed, watching as he moved to the far side of the tent and began to change his shirt. When she made no move toward her own clothing, he turned and gave her another cold look. "I said, get dressed. If you don't wish to, I'd be more than happy to return you without the charity of the clothing that I've gifted you."

Uneasy, Leah left the bed and quickly dressed in a clean chemise, ignoring the wrinkles, and laced a gown over it. Once that was done, she barely had time to do more than run her fingers through her hair when he grabbed her by the arm. "Come. We've wasted enough time." She noticed as he dragged her out of the tent that he'd dressed in a tunic so fine that she'd not seen it before. It was in the colors of his banner – blue and black – and small dragons were embroidered around the edges of his sleeves. The fabric looked to be very soft and very expensive. He'd dressed up for whoever they were going to see. Leah smoothed her hair again, worried. Was he taking her to see the king? Why would he do that?

Stumbling over her skirts and her throbbing legs, Leah had to trot to keep up with Royce's bruisingly fast pace. As he drove them through the crowd, Leah flushed with embarrassment, noting the curious looks that people gave them. She didn't have time to think too much about it, though, because they parted through the sea of tents, and she noticed that a few of Royce's men had lined up behind them, as if a protective guard. What was going on?

He stopped abruptly and she nearly crashed into his back. She stumbled to the side, dizzy with pain, and noticed that they stood in front of a portly man with a graying goatee and close-cropped hair. He was short, shorter than Leah, and his round face was florid. His tunics were rich, even if they weren't clean. Thick gold necklaces ringed his neck.

Royce thrust Leah in front of the man, and she fell to her knees at his feet. Dizzy, a flood of pain shot through her abused legs, and she barely had time to sit up and push the hair out of her face when the man began to sputter.

"What is the meaning of this, FitzWarren?" The man had a thick, blustery voice, and it slurred slightly. He was drunk, if the cup in his hand was any indicator of the situation. Wine sloshed over the edge as he staggered to his feet, splashing Leah's face. How humiliating. "How dare you show your face in my camp after taking Northcliffe from me?"

The man's words were like a splash of cold water against Leah's insides.

Oh *no*.

Lord Rutledge.

Leah looked up from the veil of hair covering her face. The expression on Royce's face was nearly unreadable. He didn't look at her, his eyes fixated on the small, dirty man that sputtered and sloshed his wine as he stepped in front of Leah.

"Answer me, FitzWarren. What is the meaning of this? Who is this wench?"

Silence fell over the small group, and after a long moment, Royce spoke. "You can cease your playacting, Rutledge. I've found out your spy, and I've come to return her to you." The coldness in Royce's voice made Leah want to cry. She remembered his voice, warm with laughter, teasing her, flirting with her. Not this stony, emotionless hatred that made her want to lie down and give up.

Baron Rutledge's rotund face turned dark red, mottled with anger. "Spy? What are you talking about?"

A quick flick of the wrist, and Royce gestured at Leah, who still sat on the grass before them, stunned and unable to react. "The wench. Your whore that you sent to seduce me."

Leah flinched at Royce's words and averted her face. Humiliation shot through her at the titters of the audience around them. *Get up and leave*, her mind whispered. *Run away from this place, away from the humiliation. He doesn't love you.*

But she needed him to love her.

Rutledge's eyes had narrowed in his face, nearly disappearing behind his cheeks. His eyes turned to her and he squinted at her, studying her rumpled appearance. Then, he turned to stare, incredulously, at Royce.

"She's yours," Royce said quietly. "I don't want to ever see her again."

The squeeze on Leah's heart lasted two moments – and that was when Baron Rutledge began to laugh, a wheezing, high-pitched sound. "You're... giving... her back?"

As Leah watched, Royce's features became even more stark with anger. "I am. Do with her as you like."

The baron erupted into more laughter. "I've never seen the whore before in my life. Did she tell you that she was mine?"

Color crept into the high cheekbones of Royce's face. "She can't talk. She's a mute."

Mocking laughter erupted from Baron Rutledge. "A mute spy? Do you think I'd take up with a mute for a mistress?" He laughed, his goblet sloshing wine all over his jerkin. Behind him, the crowd tittered, even more loudly. "The wench has taken you for a fool, FitzWarren. It's amazing you were able to wrest my keep from me, if you're felled by an ugly deaf girl."

Mute, not deaf, Leah wanted to shout, her brows furrowing with anger.

As she watched, Royce became more still than ever, though he kept his face composed. "She's not yours?"

The man just roared with laughter.

Royce turned his furious gaze on Leah, and strode over to her. She struggled to get to her feet, her movements hampered by her skirts, but before she could even get upright, she was picked up and slammed over Royce's hard shoulder. The breath whooshed out of her lungs, and she choked in silence for a long, uncomfortable moment, black swimming at the edges of her vision.

The ride was a short one, and within a span of minutes, Leah felt the tent flap brush against the back of her head and the world around her became dark as they entered the tent. That was all the warning she got before she was tossed to the pallet of blankets. She winced and opened her eyes slowly, sitting up in the bed.

Royce stared down at her with an unholy hatred in his dark eyes. His breath came from him in short rasps, and anger flushed his face. "I'll give you exactly two minutes to tell me who you are...."

Her heart breaking, Leah sadly met his eyes and gave her throat a gentle tap, shaking her head. No speaking.

A growl of rage erupted from his throat. Leah flinched and cringed back on the bed, but he didn't approach her – he flung aside a stack of equipment, scattering it across the tent. "No more lies, Leah." He turned, running his hands down his face, and she could see the line of his jaw flex with frustration. "I'm sick and tired of all the lies." He approached the side of the makeshift bed slowly, his eyes locked on her.

Leah shook her head at him and averted her eyes, unable to do anything else.

His hands were on her face in the next moment, angling her face so she could look him in the eyes. Gone was the unholy fury, replaced by a different, harder emotion. Determination. "Speak, Leah. I know you can. I heard you, down by the stream two nights ago."

Her eyes widened with surprise and she jerked away from his hands, her breath coming in short, panting gasps. He'd heard her speak? The enchantment that Muffin had her under was very strict, but eavesdropping had gotten her into trouble before. She shook her head furiously, tapping her throat in a constant, frantic reminder.

"I know the truth, Leah." His voice was deadly calm. "Tell me the real story for once – none of these fabrications that you let me assume, hiding under a veil of silence. Give me the answers I seek and I'll let you go."

But she couldn't tell him. The hard reality of his words broke Leah's shaky resolve and she buried her face in her hands, her shoulders shaking with silent sobs.

Everything was ruined. Royce would never believe her again. He wouldn't look at her with affection or tease her. He wouldn't fall in love with her in the too-short week she had left, and their final days would be spent in anger and hatred.

She'd lost everything.

Warm hands stroked her hair, and she felt lips brush a gentle kiss against her brow. "Leah," he murmured, the heartbreakingly soft tone back in his voice when he said her name. "Tell me. What are you protecting? What are you hiding with your silence?" But she couldn't speak, frustrated sobs racking her form, and for long moments, he did nothing but hold her as she wept, stroking her back and rocking her.

Unable to fight the selfish need for comfort, Leah tilted her face toward his, her lips seeking his in an urgent, frustrated kiss. She just wanted to kiss him one last time, a memory to cherish when she left with Muffin and resumed her Afterlife.

To be fair, she expected him to pull away. It would have been just what she deserved, after leading him on a string of lies that ended in his humiliation. But to her surprise, he returned her furious kiss with a response of his own. He gentled her, turning her frustration aside with slow, sensual kisses that made her want to cry anew with the tenderness of it. Softly, his lips stroked hers, easing away her fury and replacing it with a burning warmth and exultation. He wanted her. He desired her, even if he didn't love her.

She'd take it, Leah thought, as he laid her back amid the coverlets and began to touch her body. She'd take whatever scraps he'd give her, and happily, until the last time she was able to see his face.

Chapter Eighteen

When Leah woke that night, Royce was still beside her. It was pitch-dark in the tent. Beside her, Royce slept the deep, dreamless sleep of the exhausted. She sat up in bed and looked down at him, at the dark hollows ringing his eyes. He was worn through and through, and the lines of worry creasing his brow and his jaw didn't disappear tonight, even when he slept.

She was the cause of those worry lines, she knew.

He rolled over in his sleep, his back to her, and Leah breathed a small sigh of relief, easing her body carefully out of the bed. The movements made her legs protest, sending flashes of pain shooting through her limbs, flashes that she was able to blot out for the most part, quelling them by biting her lip hard enough to bleed. She dressed in her nightshift and stepped outside of the tent, instinct telling her what she would find.

Father Andrew smiled back at her, dressed in his simple, drab robes. "Shall we go someplace private to talk?"

She followed him as he led her out of the encampment, past the endless maze of tents. Lightning flashed across the sky, but not a drop rained – for which Leah was thankful. The impending storm seemed to be keeping everyone inside, for the grounds were nearly deserted at this late hour, and occasionally when they passed a tent, she'd hear the soft jumble of voices and a low-pitched laugh.

When they were a good distance away from camp, he led her underneath a tree and stepped into the shadows. Leah eyed the sky warily, remembering the flashes of lightning, but followed his lead. He smiled at her, and her nerves splintered at the sight.

"Did you find it?"

Leah feigned ignorance, even as her spine stiffened, and blinked her eyes at him.

As she watched, annoyance swiped the smug benevolence off his face. "The tithe. Did you find it?"

She shook her head. She hadn't even looked. She didn't want to look.

Father Andrew pursed his lips, his posture revealing his agitation. "You must find it. Baron Rutledge is anxious now that he knows that Royce suspects something. He plans on leaving the tourney tomorrow, and I must be with him, *with that tithe*."

He was leaving tomorrow? Oh, that was wonderful news. Leah bit her lip again to keep from smiling.

Father Andrew grabbed her by the arm. "You find this amusing, woman? Rest assured that if my plans do not work out the way I wish, I will make sure that Royce finds out your true nature, before king and all. How do you think his reputation would fare for all to learn that he had been consorting with a witch?"

Hatred swelled through her and she glared at him, fighting the urge to rub her arms from the chill he gave her. She no longer cared about her own safety, but the thought of him destroying Royce's fragile reputation was enough to bring her in line.

He grabbed her by the arm. "I'll have the tithe tomorrow?"

She nodded, and privately vowed that she'd kill him before she handed him that tithe.

The next day, Leah's legs were on fire.

It made it hard to concentrate on acting normal, and it was even more difficult when Royce pressed her body up against his and began to knead her ass, kissing her jawline. Leah's inhaled breath was taken as excitement until he touched her cheek and felt the wetness there. He recoiled as if burned.

"Why are you crying?" Royce's face transformed into all harsh angles, his eyes dark. "Does my touch disgust you now?"

She shook her head and forced a half-smile to her face, her hands clenched, fingernails digging into her palms.

He wasn't fooled. Instead, he stared at her as if she'd grown a second head. "I don't understand you, Leah. How can you be so warm to me last night, and yet this morning my touch makes you cry?"

She began to gesture, to try and somehow explain. At Royce's frustrated look, her hands dropped. She'd give anything to have her voice, to tell him the truth. Instead, she was stuck with feeble hand motions that no one understood.

Royce ignored her gesturing and glanced at the doorway to the tent. "No sign of my squire. No doubt he's nursing a hangover or still locked in the arms of some cheap whore." His eyes flicked her way. "I'll need you to help me with my armor, Leah."

She nodded and took the item he held out to her, staring at the strange, shiny piece with the leather buckles. Now how was she supposed to figure out where this went? Her fingertips touched a buckle and she studied his form, trying not to make it obvious that she had no clue as to what she was doing.

He was dressed in a thick, padded shirt that seemed too hot for the day. His leggings were dark and clung to his muscular legs, and she noticed he wore a different set of boots than he normally did. These were a thicker, darker sort. Maybe the piece of armor she held went over his boots? She glanced at the stack in the corner of the room. Each piece was wrapped in protective oilcloth, and, judging from the stack, there was quite a bit of armor to put on the man.

Leah shot a worried gaze at him. Was he jousting today? Wasn't that dangerous?

Royce laughed at the expression on her face. "Worry not. I won't die on the field today, and if I do, you'll just have to find yourself another unsuspecting male to hoodwink with your big eyes and your long legs."

She dropped the piece of armor on the ground deliberately, enjoying the angry color that flared in Royce's face.

The tent flap opened, light spilling in. Christophe entered, rubbing his eyes, his hair a mess. Leah looked at him uncomfortably and stepped away, moving back to the bedside on feet that felt like they were being sliced by razorblades.

"My lord," she heard, and winced at the scandalized tone in Christophe's voice. "She has dropped your armor in the dirt!" The ring of betrayal in his voice was loud and clear. "You should have called me." He bent over to pick up the armor piece, brushing off the shining surface with careful fingers.

Royce's lips curled up in a self-deprecating smile. "You, I'm sorry to say, were three sheets to the wind and I had no one else available. And it was me that dropped the armor. I tried to buckle it on myself, with not much luck."

"I see." The disapproving tone in the squire's voice did not change. "Allow me to help, then."

He's defending me, Leah realized, and a blush settled over her cheeks. She didn't know whether to be flattered or confused.

Leah sat down on the edge of the bed and grabbed the small embroidery hoop left out for her. It had struck her as odd yesterday that someone would have gone to all the trouble to pack her pathetic attempts at sewing, but now she was grateful for it. It gave her fingers something to do, and something for her to focus on. She watched as Christophe bent to one knee and began to strap the armor to Royce's thigh. *Well of course*, she thought sarcastically. *Obvious that it should go there.*

Royce glanced over at her, as if sensing her thoughts, and gave her a thoughtful look as the squire strapped him in. She thought she saw his lips quirk up in a smile.

The minutes ticked on in silence as Christophe took each carefully wrapped piece of armor and uncovered it, then strapped it to his waiting lord. When he took one of the heavy arm-plates and began to strap it on, he frowned and turned to Royce. "Is there something already strapped here, my lord?"

"Indeed." Royce glanced over at Leah, but she carefully averted her face, feigning disinterest, and picked at her sewing, using the needle to rip out a knot in the brightly colored embroidery thread. His voice lowered, and she saw him reach into the collar of his shirt. "I have kept the key to my lockbox safe with me at all times, though I cannot wear it during the joust. Will you keep it safe for me? I trust you with my life when I trust you with this." He handed a long, metal object to Christophe, whose features were lit up with solemn delight.

"I won't fail you, my lord," the boy promised fervently. "I've made sure to hide the box, and I'll keep the key on me at all times. No one will know that I have it."

"Good," Royce murmured. "Let us not speak of this again until it is time to give the gold to King Henry. Understood?"

The hairs on Leah's neck prickled, and she sensed both were looking over at her. Tears blurred her eyes, making her wobbly stitches even more difficult to see. So Royce didn't trust her. She wasn't surprised.

And now she knew where the tithe was. And who to steal it from.

Leah stayed in the tent the rest of the afternoon, unable to concentrate on anything. The tiny dragonflies she'd been attempting to stitch had long since gone to the wayside, and she contented herself with stitching loose, careless lettering, daydreaming and trying not to think about what she'd have to do tonight. *Leah FitzWarren*, she stitched, then frowned at it. *Lord Royce and Lady Leah*, came next, but the idea seemed so absurd and pretentious that she picked out all the stitches immediately and tossed the sewing aside.

I should be stitching Leah the Liar, or Leah the Jerk, she thought moodily. *Leah the Half-fish. Leah the Failure, soon to be permanently dead.*

She picked up the sewing and stared at it, imagining the hateful words. Could she do it? Could she betray Royce like she planned?

Leah thought for a long moment, then began to stitch.

When the light had faded too much for her to see her stitches, Leah set down her sewing and rubbed her eyes.

The tent flap opened, and Leah shoved the embroidery behind her, thrusting it under the coverlets. Her back straightened and she smoothed her hair self-consciously.

It was only Christophe. She slumped a bit to see him, disappointment sucking the breath out of her lungs.

Christophe's round face twisted in a smile. "Sorry to disappoint you, but Royce won't be returning until late tonight. He's dining with the king, and he asked me to check on you, and that I bring him..." He looked at her suspiciously. "...Something."

Something like a tithe. Leah swallowed hard, tension erupting through her body. Now was her chance. Now was her moment. The sun was low in the sky, which meant Father Andrew would return soon, and demand the tribute.

And so Leah fell to the ground, feigning a collapse, sliding in a graceless heap next to the bed.

"Leah?" Christophe's voice wavered and cracked on the last note. "Are you well?"

She forced herself to remain still, sliding her fingers around the never-used chamberpot that had been left for her convenience.

Calloused hands grabbed her by the arm and turned her over, and she blanched at the burning pain in her legs. "Mistress?" He turned her over slowly and tapped her cheek lightly, trying to waken her. "Madam?"

Her eyes slid open a crack.

He scowled at her. "'Tis a cruel trick you pull—"

She slammed the chamber pot down on his head with all the force she could muster, and a resounding 'crack' echoed in the small tent. Christophe's expression slackened, and his eyes rolled back and he collapsed on top of her.

Well, that had worked. Sort of.

174

She pried him off of her legs, sobbing silently at the bone-deep, fiery pain. No time to think about that now. Leah slid him over to the side, surprised at how heavy a man's dead weight could be. Her hands shaking at what she just did, Leah searched his body for the key.

It wasn't on him. The only thing she found were a few coins and a small, plain dagger at his belt.

She nearly burst into tears of frustration. Of course he wouldn't have it on him. If it had been her, she'd have buried it somewhere and watched it from afar. Keeping it on you meant that you left it open for others to take. What was she going to do now?

Her gaze swung to the bed, and she remembered the small pouch that held her gold belt. Father Andrew had never seen it. Joy shot through her, and she stumbled to the table on awkward, burning legs. Her fingers wrapped around the velvet bag, which she had embroidered with tiny swirls. The cord was a thick gold scrap of cording that had been too lovely to pass up.

It looked fancy. Throw in a couple of coins and a few stones, and it'd be a heavy pouch. Surely enough for a tithe of gold coin or jewelry?

Heart hammering, Leah dug through Christophe's pockets and tossed the coins she found there into the bag. It jingled a little, but the heavy weight of the necklace was comforting. She dropped a few other small items in the bag to flesh it out. A few pebbles that she found packed into the earth that made up the floor of their tent, a few buckles stolen from the remnants of Royce's armor, and within a few minutes she had a heavy, thick bag. The beautiful belt lay on top of the pile, and when she opened the bag, it winked out at her, reminding her of what she was about to do.

She didn't even have to think twice. If giving up the chain that he'd given her – that she'd cherished – meant that she could save him, she was all for it.

Leah slid her shoes on over her painfully throbbing feet and went to find Father Andrew.

She found the priest just behind a nearby tent, which was a good thing, because her legs were going to give out on her any minute. Leah stumbled toward him, breathing heavily.

"Leah?" The priest held a note of surprise in his voice. "You are here early. I had not thought you would try to get away until much later into the evening. Did you get what we seek?"

No '*how are you doing*' or '*are you well*' for her. Leah forced the wry twist of her mouth into a straight line and straightened herself, ignoring the blistering pain that it caused. Her fingers clutched the fake tithe close to her chest, and it was with feigned reluctance that she extended her hand and held it out for him to see.

Father Andrew sucked in a breath, looking at her incredulously. His fingers shook as he reached for the pouch, and glanced around furtively, as if terrified that someone would come and snatch it out of his hand. He loosened the cord and opened the bag, and Leah's heart leapt to her throat as she watched his face. Would he discover her trick?

"Marvelous," he breathed, closing the sack once more and tucking it into his belt. "You have done a wonderful job, Leah. For a time I thought you might not betray Lord Royce, since it seemed by all accounts that you were truly in love with the man, but I suppose all women are weak creatures."

Screw you, buddy, she wanted to shout, but she shook her head and gave him a small half-wave, trying to communicate that she was done with him. All she wanted now was to crawl back into Royce's bed and wait.

Leah turned away from the priest, intending to head back to her tent, and nearly bumped into a man that had come up behind her. A few other men melted from the shadows behind him, and Leah's skin began to prick nervously.

"Well, well." The voice was familiar to her, though she couldn't place her finger on it. Even more familiar, though, was the short, stocky form and the reek of old wine and unwashed skin.

"Fancy that we should meet the whore that the bastard FitzWarren has placed on high."

Baron Rutledge. Leah winced, backing away from the man. The way he stared at her made her skin crawl. A hand clasped her arm, pinning her in the spot, and Leah looked backward to stare into Father Andrew's excited face.

"She has brought us his tithe, my lord. We can break him!"

The baron's eyes bugged as he looked at Leah, then slid back into the lazy, calculating smirk. "She did? Well now, she's quite the brazen thing, given that Royce is dining with the king at the moment, and could return any minute now. Perhaps she's tired of the bastard and wants a real man in her bed." With one hand, he reached out to skim her breast.

She slapped his hand away, stumbling back against the priest. Her leg crashed into his, sending a wave of liquid agony through her body, and her knees buckled. She collapsed against the priest with a whimper.

"What's wrong with her?" The baron eyed Leah as if she had the plague. "Is she carrying FitzWarren's brat? Women are always fainting when they're with child."

Father Andrew released her quickly, stepping to the side and leaving Leah to stumble, struggling to keep upright. "I don't know if she is," he said, scandalized. "I did not think about it. She has not been sharing his bed long."

Baron Rutledge grunted. "If she is, think what that'll do to him. First, his good standing with the king, then his whore, carrying his first-born. The bastard's bastard." He roared with laughter, then glanced around furtively. "You said you had the tithe?"

"I do," the priest confirmed. "Rich necklaces and much coin. Feel how heavy the bag is." He held it out to Rutledge.

The baron hissed and waved a hand. "Keep it hidden. If Royce is still with the king, we still have time to escape before he realizes it's gone." He turned to his two guardsmen behind him. "Leave the tents, but tell the men to pack their gear. We leave in five minutes."

Leah could have cried with relief. They'd be gone and hopefully long down the road before they realized her treachery. Royce would give the king his tithe and they'd be safe. The pain in her legs was worth everything at the moment.

When the three men turned to leave, Baron Rutledge grabbed the closest one by the arm. "You. Stay." The baron glanced over at Leah, who stood off to the side, wilting. "Take the sick wench and put her on one of the horses."

"My lord," Father Andrew said, a hint of worry in his normally sweet voice. "Are you sure that is wise? The wench cannot tell Lord FitzWarren where we have gone – I do not think it would be a problem to leave her behind."

Leah's captor overpowered her, and even though she struggled, she was flung over the man's shoulder. Her legs thrashed as she tried to get away, only to have the man put a tight, confining arm over her legs that made her shudder with a new wave of pain.

"On the contrary, my dear priest. This could not work out more perfectly." Baron Rutledge stepped to the side, ignoring Leah's heaving form. "The bastard will think that she's gone and stolen his money and run away with me… just as he always feared. Did he not fling the wench at my feet, thinking she was a traitor? He'll place the blame at her pretty feet and by the time he's able to get the wench back, we'll have his bastard son in tow. And he can pay a fine ransom for him, as well." His evil giggle floated through the air. "Now come. We must leave, and fast."

The man holding Leah jostled her, hard, and his hand slapped her rump. The pain that flared through her body was great enough that blackness swam at the edges of her vision, and she tumbled into darkness.

Chapter Nineteen

The first thing that Royce noticed when he returned to his tent was that Leah was gone. The bed was rumpled but empty, and the rest of the tent was untouched. There was a plate of dinner sitting on a nearby makeshift table that was congealed and covered in flies. No doubt it had been there for several hours.

Unease pricked along his nerve endings, and he shot a quick glance through the darkened tent, wondering if he'd overlooked her. "Leah?" He wondered if this was a trick of hers, to frighten him, and he'd turn around and see her beautiful, pale face smiling up at him from underneath the thick fringe of mahogany hair. Her green eyes would light up at the sight of him and the pretty fabrics he'd wavered on, until he finally broke down and bought them for her as an apology for the way he'd been acting. He wanted to see her dressed in nice things. It didn't matter that she couldn't – wouldn't – talk to him. He'd coax her and romance her into being comfortable with him on all levels and then she'd speak, and he'd learn all the secrets about her that plagued his sleep, even as her soft skin plagued his daydreams.

Heavens help him, but he was acting like a schoolboy with a woman he couldn't even trust.

A groan in the far corner of the tent caught his attention, and Royce stormed through the tent, seeking its source. His heart froze in his chest at the sight of the crumpled form lying next to the bed, and he knelt, turning the figure over.

One quick touch made him immediately realize it was not Leah. The smell of sweat covered the slumped form, and the second groan that followed was decidedly male.

"Royce?" The figure mumbled on the floor.

"Christophe," he said, his unease clenching tighter and tighter. "What has happened to Leah? Who has taken her?"

The squire sat up, his hand going to his head. "Leah?" He said, his thought slow and confused.

"Yes," Royce said, trying not to shout at the boy. "Leah is gone. Did you see anyone in the tent? Who hit you?"

Incredulous, the squire stared up at Royce. "Why, my lord, she did."

It didn't make sense, Royce thought as he paced his tent. He'd gathered several of his men nearby and questioned them. It didn't make an ounce of blasted sense.

Leah had knocked his squire out – the only one with the key to his precious tithe that he owed the king. The tithe that would allow him to keep Northcliffe despite the uncouth way he had retaken it. The tithe that meant everything.

At first, he'd assumed she'd stolen it, and his heart nearly turned to ice in his chest.

But then Christophe had produced the key, and the tithe.

She hadn't stolen it after all. A quick search of her possessions showed that she'd left all her things behind –

her gowns, her cloak, even her sewing. The only thing she'd taken was her necklace that he'd given her.

So she'd needed money.

He thought back to the voice he'd heard her talking to, several nights ago. The voice that still played in his mind.

"But... I love him." Leah had said, her head pillowed on her knees by the shore of the small stream. Her hair had been wet, and she was dressed in a damp shift that clung to her form. Seductive clothing. Clothing that only a lover should see her in. Her words had ended in a broken half-sob. *"I never thought this would be so hard. What am I going to do if I can't make him love me? I have to. It's what I came here to do."*

The other voice hadn't cared about her agony.

"Well, I must go. I've a certain someone to meet up with, and he doesn't like to be kept waiting," he remembered the other saying, and could have sworn the other voice was female. But that didn't make sense.

Why would Leah be meeting with another woman and pouring out her heart to her?

Why would she attack his squire and run from him? If she was working for Baron Rutledge, why wouldn't she take the tithe if she had the opportunity?

He sat down on the bed heavily, wading through the random stream of thoughts that blasted through his mind. Leah's smiling, happy face back in his castle. Her drawn, pensive look when the smithy burned down. Her sad eyes on the journey, as if she knew something was terribly wrong and couldn't say anything. And always, always that damned priest, watching her with avid, interested eyes. Always at her elbow, guiding her or giving her advice.

The priest.

Lost in thought, he almost didn't notice the small flare of pain searing his buttock, until he shifted again and the needle slid into his skin. "Ow!" Royce jumped up and turned to the bed, searching through the covers for the culprit, and his hands found Leah's small embroidery hoop, the needle carelessly pointing up from the cloth.

It didn't look like most women's stitchery. There were no decorative curls, no ornate lettering – the stitches here were quick and messy, strung out in a pattern that could only be writing. He held it up to his nose, smelling the faintly salty perfume that always seemed to accompany Leah's possessions.

"A candle," Royce called, turning over the stitching in his hand. When one was provided, he held it up to the pale, thin cloth.

It was full of lettering. Words she'd strung together. The characters were sloppy, some more than others, as if she found the lettering strange. Across the top of the embroidery, he saw a careful set of alphabetic letters, a second set of similar, if odd-looking characters crawling beneath it. Like she didn't know the language, and had tried to match it up to her own.

All so she could leave him a message.

I'm sorry, it read, the stitches sloppy, rushed. *Never betrayed you. Be wary of the priest. Always loved you.*

There was more stitching at the bottom that had been carefully picked out, but the holes fell into an easy-to-read pattern. Her name, Leah, and a longer set of pulled stitches, with a double-f. Northcliffe. She'd daydreamed about taking his name.

Never betrayed you. Be wary of the priest.
Always loved you.

The thin, pale fabric was spattered with slightly darker rings across the fabric. Watermarks, leaving faint stains on the fragile fabric from her tears.

"Where is the priest?" He scarcely recognized the hoarse voice as his own.

"We cannot find him, my lord."

He had been betrayed.

And a short time later, when it was reported that Baron Rutledge was missing, he knew what had happened.

And what he was going to do.

"You've worked yourself into a real mess now, haven't you?" Muffin's thready voice whispered in Leah's ear.

Leah's eyes slid open and she peered into the darkness. Even that slight movement caused a slither of remembered pain to shoot through her. She blinked several times, trying to focus her mind. She was sure that she'd heard Muffin's voice, but looking around, she didn't see anything or anyone.

A patch of fleshy grass lay under her cheek, and the cold dew soaked under her cheek. She guessed she'd been left there while the men took a quick break – they were active and talking, moving about camp, even though it was pitch-black outside. Her hands were bound behind her, but loosely. Her feet were untied. Just as well. She wouldn't be escaping with the condition her body was in and they knew it.

Leah smacked her lips, a terrible taste in her mouth, and tried her voice. "Muffin? I can't see you."

"Look down," said Muffin again, and Leah did.

On a nearby blade of grass, something moved. At first, Leah thought it was a bug. It was certainly the right size – but then it twitched, and Leah caught a flounce of blue skirts and white sausage curls. It was Muffin, her body shrunk down to the size of a penny.

"Surprise!" She beamed at Leah and poked the tip of her nose with a teeny sparkling wand. "Bet you didn't expect to see me here. Now what on earth are you up to with these terrible men?"

Leah lifted her head slightly and glanced around. No one was paying attention to her, the men focused on the food and a few private conversations that would probably curl her toes if she could hear them. She nestled her cheek back in the grass and turned back to Muffin. "I've been captured by Royce's enemy. Baron Rutledge."

"Hmm." Muffin tapped her wand against her chin, considering this. "That could put a definite kink in your plans. Why don't you run away?"

"Legs," she said, and the very word made them throb. "Hurt. Haven't been in the ocean in days."

Instead of the sympathy she normally received from the fairy godmother, Muffin tsked and shook her head. "Not very well done of you, I'm afraid. So what do you plan to do to fix it? You've only got four days left."

Only four? Despair overwhelmed Leah. She'd never see Royce again. "It doesn't matter. I've failed. He doesn't love me. I'm not long for this world anyway. When Baron Rutledge finds out that I've lied to him, he's going to kill me."

Muffin pursed her lips. "I can't help you, Leah. I wish I could, but that would go against the fairy godmother conventions, and I'd be fired if I let that happen. I'm sorry." She reached out one tiny hand and patted Leah's cheek. "You're going to have to stick it out for a few more days."

Unable to speak past the knot of disappointment forming in her throat, Leah nodded. She'd take the days, even with the blinding pain. Every moment left here was another chance that she might see Royce again.

Just then, a loud, angry bellow swelled from the makeshift camp. Muffin blinked out of existence, and Leah winced.

If she had to make a bet, she'd guess that Baron Rutledge had found the fake tithe. When his fingers wrapped around her throat and he began to scream in her face, she knew she'd guessed right.

"You little bitch," he yelled. "Where is the real tithe?"

Air suddenly became a precious commodity as his hands choked her throat. She struggled against him, but she was weak from pain, plus her hands were still tied. She started seeing stars and a harsh buzzing began at the base of her skull.

He released her at some point, when time had ceased to be anything but a vacuum without air, when things popped and burst behind her eyes and she began to think she'd get to Heaven a little faster than she and Muffin had anticipated. But then he released her, and air rushed back into her wounded throat in one thick, cold rush.

"No matter," Baron Rutledge hissed, leaning over her. She felt hot droplets of spittle splash across her cheek as he spoke. "Royce will come after his little whore, regardless of whether or not we have his riches. And think how it will hurt him to see what I've done to you. I think you'll be a lot less charming to him with fewer teeth. Unless you speak up now, of course."

Leah smiled, the muscles in her neck protesting. Her tongue felt thick, and she could have laughed in his face. Even if she could talk, she would never reveal anything that would harm Royce. Blackmail or not.

Rutledge seemed to sense this, and as she watched, his face became mottled and red with fury. His fist rose into the air, and she saw it swing down just before the bone-jarring impact hit her and she lost consciousness, falling into a blessed, pain-free sleep.

Chapter Twenty

By the time the smell of the ocean hit Leah's nostrils again, she was nearly insensible with pain. Pain from her bruised face and throbbing head, pain from her throat that felt like it had been ripped open, pain from her legs that overrode everything else and reminded her of her curse. A guardsman had been assigned to her when she'd slid off of the horse for the third time, and now she was cradled against the chest of a thick, sweaty man who smelled like he hadn't bathed since Christmas.

Even his stench couldn't keep out the scent of the ocean. It roused her from her stupor and made her lift her head. The salty breeze was coming from the west, and she turned her head toward it, her mouth salivating at the thought of release from the agony. Her blurry gaze focused in on a familiar crop of rocky stone, and the sight caused her to gasp with despair.

Northcliffe was on the horizon.

Baron Rutledge would win after all.

Hot, disappointed tears slid down Leah's face. She'd thought for sure that something would happen – that Royce would arrive just in time, that Baron Rutledge would turn around – that something would happen to stop this terrible turn of events.

It hadn't. As the cool stone gates of Northcliffe loomed ever closer, Leah's heart sank in her chest.

Baron Rutledge's soldiers were encouraged by the sight of the doors, and a low cheer rose from the men. She heard Rutledge laughing with his delight as he spurred his horse forward. "We'll retake the keep from the bastard's grip! He'll learn not to cross me again!"

To Leah's horror, the portcullis was up. Were the people of Northcliffe insane? Weren't they aware that Baron Rutledge was riding back to retake the keep? Once he was behind the walls again, they'd never be able to dig him out.

She thought of herself and Royce. Helpless tears tracked down the side of her face again, and she closed her eyes, turning her face toward the ocean once more, hoping for a soothing breeze.

Which was why she was so startled when the horses riding through the portcullis stopped.

Leah opened her eyes and stared at the semi-circle of mounted soldiers ahead of them, fifty strong and turned out in shining armor. Somehow, impossibly, Royce's men were in the courtyard, prepared and ready.

Royce stood at the head of the line, raising his sword blade to his brow in a mocking salute to Baron Rutledge.

"Welcome to my home, Rutledge."

As she watched, Baron Rutledge jerked on the reins of his horse, the animal turning skittishly in place. "This is my keep, FitzWarren. I come to claim what is rightfully mine."

"As have I." The cool, careless voice made Leah's pulse skitter, and she sucked in a breath as Royce's dark eyes searched the crowd, seeking a familiar face. Hers. She knew when his gaze touched her. An electric pulse of longing shot through her, and, as she watched, a muscle clenched in his jaw. "I see you are rough with your toys,

Rutledge, but I suppose that should come as no surprise to me, given how I found the state of my ancestral home."

Rutledge laughed, a mocking, bitter sound. "You can't fool me, FitzWarren. You've come after the whore because you're in love with her. I should have guessed that like blood seeks like," he sneered. "It seems we are at an impasse. I have what you want, and you have what I want."

"Let us finish this, then." Royce said quietly. "A duel. You and me. Winner takes all."

"If I defeat you, I will hang your corpse from the rafters of this castle."

"If it suits you." Royce sounded toneless, bored. It puzzled Leah. She'd never known Royce to be so calm and unruffled. "Know that I shall do the same with you, should I win."

He would win. Of that, Leah had no doubt. Baron Rutledge was a short, portly man who looked like he'd been living on the hard edge of life for some time. Royce, on the other hand, was well formed with broad shoulders, and he fairly glowed with health. He also vibrated with anger. It charged the air around them and gave him an intensity that Rutledge lacked.

It seemed stupid for Rutledge to agree to this. She didn't understand. As she watched, the two lords stepped forward, each unsheathing his sword. As one, the men circling them – on both sides of this feud – stepped back to allow the fighters room.

The baron twitched one of his fingers as he stepped forward, and Leah's eyes were drawn to that subtle movement. Hers were not the only ones; the man in charge of holding her shifted, and the next thing she knew, she was being thrust from his horse into Father Andrew's arms. "Take the wench," the man growled, just as the first clang of swords pierced the air.

Father Andrew's arms clutched at her waist desperately, and he struggled to keep his balance atop his mule. Once he got her situated, he stared at the battlefield ahead. Leah couldn't see much except the occasional flash of a blade before the crowd cheered wildly – on Royce's side. He was winning! Her heart soared.

"What are you doing?" Father Andrew's quiet voice caught her attention. She turned, following his gaze.

The soldier was carefully raising a small crossbow in the jut of his arm, squinting down the stock. "Baron's orders," he muttered. As she watched, he loaded the crossbow and angled the tip of it, following Royce's movements. "Can't have the bastard keeping the castle from Baron Rutledge, can we?"

No! Leah acted before she could think; she flung herself at the man's horse, fists pummeling. He would not kill Royce by cheating! He would not!

The horse squealed in surprise as Leah slammed into the side of it, saddle-buckles and the soldier's boot digging into her ribs before the breath whooshed out of her lungs. She heard the sickening twang as the crossbow fired and time slowed...

As her horrified eyes watched, the man in front of them slumped on his horse, then tumbled forward, the crossbow bolt sticking out of his back. One of the men called out in outrage, and one of Royce's men pointed and shouted. "Cheater! He cheats!"

The cry took up in the courtyard, and soon it echoed with the sound of the outraged men. Swords were drawn, and suddenly the neat semi-circle had given way to a madhouse of angry men, and the clang of swords increased tenfold.

Leah wobbled on her feet, momentarily confused. She had saved Royce, but she'd also made things worse.

Firm, grasping fingers latched onto her upper arm. "Come with me," Father Andrew hissed. At some point, he had gotten off of his mule and was now at her side.

Leah shook her head furiously and shrugged out of his grasp. She didn't want to go with him – she wanted to stay and see Royce.

"I'll take you to the ocean – just come with me!"

Leah hesitated. Another loud call from the fray before them, and she paused, her anxious eyes scanning the crowd for a familiar dark head. She couldn't see Royce anywhere in the tangle of flashing arms and swords.

A wiry arm wrapped around her and dragged her backward, too strong for her to overpower in her weakened state. "If you won't go willingly, I'm going to have to force you to come with me, my dear," the priest said, pulling her toward his waiting mule. Pain shot through her arm, and she stumbled along with him.

Away from the battle.

Away from Royce.

She wanted to cry from the pain – not from her body, but from her heart. Royce was out there in the midst of that terrible melee, and Baron Rutledge was trying to kill him by any means necessary. She wanted to see him – wanted to be with him, even if it was for his last moments, and hers as well. Leah flailed in protest, and the priest kicked her legs in response, his frustration erupting. Pain blossomed through her and she collapsed. He shoved her onto his mule, then climbed up behind her and spurred the animal forward.

The long, winding path to the rocky shoreline seemed to go on forever and the slow, jarring gait of the mule was unhurried. Leah rolled in and out of consciousness, the priest's wiry arm wrapped tightly across her neck, pinning her against him and making it hard to breathe through an already wounded throat.

Salty, tangy air filled her nostrils with every step closer to the beach, causing her leg muscles to clench in anticipated response. Her breathing became more shallow, as if even her lungs were excited about the prospect of a release from pain.

Worry overrode everything in her mind – worry for Royce, not for herself. She didn't care if the priest was kidnapping her as insurance for himself, or if there was a fouler motive. She just wanted to know that Royce was safe.

"Faster, faster," the priest breathed against Leah's neck, urging the mule forward as they descended onto the sandy beach. "We must go faster. If he catches us, we are both lost." Fear clouded his voice, and she could feel his thin form trembling against her own.

Not me, she wanted to shout. *Royce will save me*! She struggled against his arm, and bit down on the pale flesh near her mouth. Her teeth sank into the meat of his arm, and she ground down until she tasted blood.

Father Andrew howled in anguish. "Foul witch!" He shook his arm, trying to dislodge her. His arm smacked into her face several times, but she refused to let go until his fingers pried her mouth open. She spat the blood at him and shook her head, trying to clear it of the ringing pain and the taste of unwashed priest. "I'm trying to help you, you foul creature," he snarled in her ear and clamped his fingers on her chin, forcing her to stare ahead at the ocean that lapped at the mule's hooves. "I will release you to the ocean, but you must promise never to come back. Never to tell Lord Royce what has happened here or I shall blame it all on you and expose your secret." His whisper-soft words were nearly drowned out in the roar of the ocean against her ears. It covered all, soothing her with the soft wake and the sound of the tide, of the splashing as the water hit the mule's hooves. The cry of seagulls overhead. Longing, physical, wrenching longing shot through her, and she trembled with the force of it.

"Take your hands off of her."

The calm, deadly voice pierced Leah's ears with the thunder of a lightning storm. Royce! Her heart swelled, and she jerked free of the priest's restraining hands, craning her neck to look at him, unholy joy shooting through her body.

Royce was almost twenty feet away from them, a good distance back on the beach. As she watched, he slid from his mount and slowly strode forward, a noticeable hitch in his step and blood soaking the front of his dark tunic. There was an ugly gash on his forehead, and his dark hair was plastered to his head in sweaty curls. And he looked absolutely furious. His hand clenched his sword tightly, and he continued striding toward the priest. "You'll take your hands off her right now—"

"Stop!" Father Andrew's sweet voice had taken on a nervous, high-pitched whine. "Stop or you'll force me to do something I'll regret!"

To her surprise, Royce halted, his dark eyes never swerving from her face. With one glance, he caressed her body, noted every bruise on her face, the gouges on her neck, all a tender appraisal that said he cared. "Let her go," he repeated, though his words were calmer now than before. "It's over. Baron Rutledge is dead."

"I knew he would be," the priest said. "You're the true lord of the castle. Everyone knows it."

"Then why betray me?" His eyes didn't lift from Leah's bruised face. "Why steal what is mine and try and give it to my enemy?"

Warmth flushed her tense, trembling body. His low, even words were for her as much as the priest. He was telling her that he knew it wasn't her fault. That he wanted her. Hot tears of relief slid down her cheeks.

"I am helping you, my lord," Father Andrew said, his voice taking on a dangerous tone. "Please, step away. Return to the castle and let me finish this in peace."

Finish? Leah wondered at his words.

Something hard and cold pricked at her throat. She tensed, her eyes becoming wild with fear. Her throat flexed and she felt the hard tip of a knife digging into her bruised skin. "Back away, my lord," the priest said softly. "I do this for you, so you may see that my motives are pure."

The look on Royce's face became shuttered, frozen. His eyes dragged from Leah's to stare into the priest's with hate. "If you harm her, I'll skin you alive."

"She has you under her spell," Father Andrew explained in a calm, unholy voice. "God has shown me that I must break you from her hold. It is the only way to salvation."

Oh no. Oh no no no.

The priest's hand moved, as if in slow motion, and as Leah watched, Royce sprang forward. She felt the knife dig into her throat, felt it pierce her skin, felt the world tilt on its axis as the priest was jerked away from her. Without his slender weight to support her aching body, she tipped over the side of the mule and fell down...

Straight into the rushing, ebbing tide that beat against the sandy shore.

Her entire body clenched as the freezing waters slid over her legs, soaking her skirts immediately. Then, with an almost unholy joy, her entire body convulsed, and she began to transform right then and there. Helpless, Leah curled her arms around her body and waited for the intense mix of pain and unburdened relief to finish sweeping through her system. The waves beat against her as her lungs expelled the air trapped inside them, her gills separated and formed, and her legs molded together, becoming a strong, powerful tail that had been suppressed for far too long.

In front of Royce. She'd transformed in front of Royce, despite all her careful precautions.

Somewhere in the distance, beyond the roar of the ocean and the roar of her own blood, she heard the priest laughing maniacally. "See? See! What did I tell you, my lord! Witchcraft!"

Her painful transformation finished, Leah struggled to sit upright, but all she could manage was to lift her torso, propping herself up on her elbows as the waves of the ocean beat against her, over and over again. Dully, she stared up at the two men. Father Andrew had a look of triumph on his face.

The look on Royce's face?

Aghast. Shocked. Betrayed.

Humiliated, Leah smoothed the hair from her face and tried to speak. "I'm sorry," she wanted to say, but nothing came out of her mouth except a lonely squeak. Frustrated, she clenched her fist and pounded it against the grainy sand. She wanted to explain herself to him, to explain the fact that she couldn't breathe because the dress was sticking to her gills, that her tail was flicking of its own accord, muscles twitching with relief.

She saw his gaze trail to her flickering tail, then he paled and shook his head. She had her answer. He'd found out her secret and had not declared love for her. She'd lost the game. It felt like her heart was breaking in her chest.

Heartbroken, Leah turned and slid out into the water, hurrying away from the shore, away from the accusing eyes that stared at her as if she was a freak.

Running away from her failures and the loss of a love that she was never supposed to have in the first place. The ocean soothed her soul, drowned her tears, and relieved the burning pain that she had found so familiar in the past few days.

But it couldn't undo the pain in her heart.

The final three days of her ordeal passed surprisingly quickly for Leah.

At first, there was the mindless torment that numbed her heart and made her soul ache. The pain that forced her brain to replay, over and over again, the shocked, horrified look on Royce's face when he stared at her twitching tail. The priest's exultation. Royce's horror. Over and over again, and the entire time, she cried silent tears into the caressing, enclosing waves of the ocean.

When her heart was numb and she couldn't think any more, she let the waves carry her. She welcomed the dark, stormy depths of the ocean. Far out to sea she went, then ventured back to land when the waters became too deep and the creatures that lived there were much, much larger than herself.

The longer she retained her mermaid form, the more blurred her mind became. It was as if having the tail somehow turned off part of her brain and allowed her to focus just on the visceral world around her – the world that she'd be pulled from in just a few short hours.

She'd failed, and she'd be sent on from this earth, the earth with the dark, salty ocean full of swimming, breathing, teeming life. And she swam, not even surfacing to the air once during those three days, living as the fish live, and letting it numb her mind. With air came memories, and she wanted to forget.

She *did* forget, for a time, but her dreams were haunted by dark eyes, betrayed and full of horror, and Leah would wake up with an aching throat and irritated eyes and know that she'd been crying, even underwater.

So she sank deeper into mermaid consciousness, that
half-awareness that left her only cognizant of her tail
flicking through the deep waters and the pull of her gills
against the icy ocean waters.

Until, at some point, the pinching began.

At first, she ignored it, thinking it was a muscle
cramp. The pain was a slight throbbing at the base of her
tail, insignificant compared to the pain she had endured
previously. But it continued, growing stronger and
sharper by the minute, until she was doubled over in the
water, struggling to swim. She flipped over onto her
back, belly facing the sky, and to her surprise, the pain
abated slightly. Taking that as a cue, Leah began to
swim upward, just a flick ahead of the rapidly increasing
agony.

The pain disappeared the moment her head broke the
surface. She squinted at the late afternoon sunlight,
eyeing the sky with trepidation. It burned her eyes after
the cool, wet darkness of the ocean the past few days.

"There you are! I was starting to wonder if I'd ever
find you again." Muffin's thin voice was reedy with
disapproval. "You are a hard lady to find once you get
beneath that water, do you know that? I've been pinching
your tail for hours now, and you've just now noticed. I
was starting to think I'd have to come in after you!" She
fanned herself with a gloved hand.

Leah turned to Muffin and squinted at her. The fairy
godmother was dressed in another one of her outfits, this
one a striped Victorian bathing ensemble, complete with
a frilly parasol perched over one shoulder. A flowered
swim cap clung to her head. It irritated Leah to see her
so chipper in the wake of her own mindless pain.

"Are we done here? Is it time to go?" Her voice was
dull, but Leah didn't care. Disappointment clouded
through her at the sight of the fairy godmother, and she
knew that these would be her last moments on earth.

Sure, Heaven was supposed to be paradise, but she still felt somehow... cheated out of a normal life.

Cheated out of a normal life, she thought bitterly. *That's rich, coming from a woman cursed to be a mermaid.*

"Not just yet, I'm afraid," Muffin said cheerily. "You haven't exactly wrapped things up here, you know."

Leah resisted the urge to splash water in her face. "What do you mean? Isn't this enough?" Her hand slapped the surface, causing a shockwave of ripples on the already rough waters. "I failed. You gave me a task, and I failed it. What more do you want from me?"

Muffin inclined her head, a subtle gesture at the bright strip of shore that lay far back in the distance. A smile curved her lips, blissfully sweet and unaware of Leah's resentment. "It's not me, my dear. There's a man that's been standing on that shore for three days now, rain, shine, day, night. I think he deserves some sort of explanation, don't you?"

Her heart thudded to a stop in her breast, and Leah forced herself to slowly turn and examine the strip of beach that she'd previously ignored.

She was so far out to sea that it was hard to make out anything at all, but her straining eyes caught a dark figure near the water's edge, and a flash of blue that was the exact shade of Royce's favorite tunic.

Leah's mouth went dry, and she turned to Muffin. Her eyes were wide with uncertainty. "I can't, Muffin. I can't talk to him."

"Why?" Muffin wrinkled her nose. "He was good enough to sleep with, but not good enough to talk to now that he knows that you're part fish?"

Her pert words humiliated Leah, and she fought the urge to sink back under the water. The fairy godmother would be disappointed by her cowardice. She blinked rapidly, trying to force away the moisture pooling in her

198

eyes. "I… I don't know. I'm afraid of what he'll say to me." The words caused her throat to close up, and she swallowed hard, then glanced at her fairy godmother again. "You didn't see the way he looked at me. Like I was… some unnatural creature. He was disgusted."

"But, my dear, you *are* an unnatural creature. Allow the man to be shocked." She snapped her parasol shut and turned her face up to the sun. "We've got a little bit of time before the sun sets, so you might as well go over and get it done with." She leaned down toward Leah. "I know you're scared, but take it from an old lady – the man's been looking for you for three days. I think something more urgent is on his mind than whether or not your tail is repulsive."

Fear warred with regret and longing. She wanted to see him one last time, no matter how much it might hurt. Even if her last view of him was the disgust written on his face, she still wanted to look into those dark eyes one more time.

Without glancing back at Muffin, she began to swim toward the beach. As she moved through the water, she kept her eyes on the shoreline. Gradually, it came into focus, and she could see Royce standing on the shore. His arms were crossed over his chest, his gaze focused on the ocean. She knew he was looking for her, because when he noticed the top of her head as she swam in closer, his large body stiffened and he took a few steps forward.

Leah faltered, but forced herself to continue. *One hand in front of the other, flick your tail, eyes forward. It'll all be over soon, and then you'll never see him again. Never see him again.*

Her throat closed and a fresh round of tears threatened. She didn't want to leave him. Even if he hated her, she'd gladly stay in his castle, all so she could look at him every day. Leah cursed the selfishness of the past three days – days that she had hidden from him and the world. It was time she could have spent at his castle, with him, no matter how painful the end result would be. She'd cheated herself out of it, like a stupid fool.

The water became shallow enough that she had to pull herself forward with her arms across the sand, dragging her heavy tail onto the beach. She didn't know why, but the water felt like a barrier between them.

She knew she'd come far enough in, because her gills seized up and began to burn, and her tail clenched. Leah collapsed on the ground as the transformation took over her body, her lungs forcing the water from them and her legs searing as they split apart once more. She hid her face from him. He'd be disgusted by her rough transformation.

Gentle hands slid under her waist, holding her as if she might break. Fingers brushed the hair off of her face, wet with salt-water and tears. "Leah," Royce whispered, and her heart clenched in a completely different kind of pain. "Don't cry. It's all right, Leah."

The tears poured forth then, as if a dam had burst. She sobbed, turning her face against his chest so he couldn't see the pain in her eyes. All the while he stroked her hair and cradled her body against his.

"Please don't cry, Leah." His thumb brushed away the tears under her eyes. "I can't stand to see you cry." She felt his lips brush against her forehead. "We don't have to tell anyone about this."

Leah tensed in his arms, not following his logic. What did he mean, not tell anyone? Not tell anyone about what? Curious, she opened her eyes and looked into his face.

Warm, dark eyes stared down into her face as if he were trying to memorize her features. Royce looked exhausted, Leah realized. Dark circles ringed his eyes, and his face was drawn, his hair a tousled mess. He looked like he hadn't slept in days. More real than his exhaustion, however, was the tenderness with which he looked at her.

"I've sent Father Andrew away, Leah. Back to his monastery, where he can't spill his secrets or use them against you." He touched the edge of her jaw with gentle, reverent fingers. "We won't tell anyone about your secret, Leah. I'll get a secret passage built in my chambers, so you can come to the ocean as often as you need to. You can do whatever you like. Just don't run away again."

Her face crumpled at his sweet words. He was being so kind and understanding – he didn't hate her at all. Didn't think she was a monster. She hated that she'd left him for the past three days, thinking that he'd been tainted by Father Andrew's vicious lies and fear-mongering. She could have spent three more days in his arms. And now it was too late. She buried her face in his neck, inhaling the musky scent of him, awash in bitter regret.

He cradled her closer to him, as if sensing the tension rampant in her body. "At first I was angry you had kept the secret from me, Leah, but then Father Andrew kept going on about devil-spawn, and I realized you were afraid that I'd cast you aside, or worse." His hands tightened around her body. "I'd never do that to you, Leah." His fingers reached under her chin and he tilted her head so she would look up at him. His eyes caressed her face, devouring her sad features. "It's all right. You'll come to trust me, eventually. We'll get married, and you'll be lady of my keep, and no one will force you to do anything you don't want to ever again. My men will treat you with respect, and the servants already love you. And I know you can talk, but there must be a reason why you won't talk to me. You'll come to trust me, eventually, and then you can tell me everything. But I'll wait until you're ready."

Oh god. Her heart was breaking now. She couldn't stop crying, even as she touched his face, bringing his lips down to hers for one last, bittersweet kiss. His lips touched hers softly, as if he were afraid of breaking her. "Leah, Leah. Stay with me forever."

But she couldn't. Leah pulled away, shaking her head, and placed her fingers on his lips. She couldn't stay, and her gaze strayed out to the ocean again.

"I don't understand," he began, but his words died when a shadow fell over the two of them.

Muffin rapped him on the head with her parasol. "I'm afraid it's time for us to go, young man."

She felt him stiffen against her, felt him surge to his feet, still cradling her against his chest. "Who are you?" he demanded, his voice harsh with fear.

"Leah's keeper," Muffin said in a truculent voice. "She had a task to do, and she failed. Now I'm afraid it's time for her to go. Say your goodbyes."

His arms tightened around Leah. "You don't have to go anywhere, sweetling. You can stay with me." His whispered words brushed against her ear, making her heart swell with emotion.

She shook her head, pulling his arms away from her and stepping out of his grip, even though every fiber of her body was screaming for her to run back to his arms. Leah touched his cheek gently by apology, then bowed her head, turning to follow the waiting Muffin.

"Leah, wait!" Royce grabbed her arm. "I don't understand what's going on." Anger rushed through his voice. "You're just going to leave again?"

She shook her head sadly, and pointed at the ocean. She wanted to tell him that she had no choice. Remembering Muffin's presence, Leah cleared her throat and experimented. "I..." Her breath whooshed out of her lungs in relief that she could speak. "My voice. It's back!"

"So you couldn't speak?"

"No. Only around Muffin. Oh Royce, I'm so sorry. I can't stay with you. It's too late for that." Her hand slid out of his and she continued to walk forward, her head bowed. Her vision blurred with hot tears, and she forced herself to keep walking forward.

"It'll all be over soon," Muffin soothed, putting an arm around her waist.

Inconsolable, Leah turned away and faced the ocean. Muffin's little boat still bobbed out in the distance. She could swim out to it, she supposed, and then it would all end once she was out of Royce's sight.

To Leah's surprise, Muffin's arm was ripped from her waist, and the fairy godmother was tossed aside. Warm hands grasped Leah, pulling her against a hard, familiar body, and she looked into Royce's hard, unsmiling mouth and grim eyes.

"Tell me that you want this, and I'll leave you be, Leah. Tell me that you don't want to stay, and I'll let this go."

She touched his cheek gently, ignoring the sputtering of the fairy godmother behind them. "It's not that I don't want to stay, Royce," she said, her voice husky with lack of use. "It's that I don't have a choice."

His free hand slid behind her neck, and he pressed his forehead against hers in a gesture that brought new tears to her eyes. "Then know this before you leave." He pressed a crumpled bit of thread and fabric into her hand, and Leah stared down at the mangled embroidery she'd left in his tent. *I always loved you*, the tearstained cloth read, mocking her.

"I always loved you as well," Royce said, and kissed her once, then released her.

The world stilled around them.

"Oh crap," Muffin said, with disgust. "Just under the wire, eh? Typical man." She gave a huge sigh.

A hot flash of pain throbbed through Leah's legs, a wholly unique sort of pain that she hadn't felt before. Alarmed, Leah fell against Royce and clung to his tunic as her limbs stiffened in response.

The world began to roar around her, and darkness threatened to overcome her, but it wasn't a painful sort of blackness – rather, it was like her body was building up, preparing for something huge.

And then it stopped, just as suddenly as it started.

Surprised, Leah opened one eye experimentally, and squinted at the world around her. She could feel Royce's arm under her legs, and the rest of her was cradled against his chest again. He must have hauled her up in his arms while she was nearly blacked out from pain. The look in his eyes as he stared down at her was as confused as her own. Both of them turned to Muffin.

The fairy godmother gave them a sweet smile. "Well, I suppose I'll have to make other arrangements after all." She waved her wand in Leah's direction. "You're free to go, my girl."

"I am? I'm free of the fish tail?" Her hands clenched in the fabric of Royce's tunic, unable to believe that her luck would turn so fast. "Really?"

"Indeed you are," the fairy godmother crowed. "Did you want to go back to Seattle now?"

She felt Royce's arms tighten protectively around her, and Leah clung to his neck, trying to back away from the fairy godmother and her horrible suggestion. "Oh no! I want to stay here!"

"That wasn't part of the original deal." She waved her wand at Leah chidingly. "However, given that your young man looks ready to take my head off at the thought of you leaving again, I suppose we can leave things like they are, if that would make you happy."

Leah reached up and kissed Royce's cheek, hardly daring to hope. "Nothing would make me happier," she whispered.

The fairy godmother made a puking noise. "Spare me the sappy stuff, my dear. Very well. You can stay, but I don't want to have to see your face again for another sixty years at least, do you hear me?"

She grinned. "Loud and clear."

Muffin winked and gave her a quick salute with the wand. "That's it then. I'm done here. Have a nice life, kiddo." And just like that, she winked out of existence. Far out in the distance, Leah saw the tiny white boat vanish.

Just like that, it was over. Leah turned to Royce, still feeling slightly shell-shocked. He wasn't moving, just staring down at her with the same incredulous expression on his face, like he'd seen too much to digest in one sitting.

She pinched him.

That woke him up, and he quirked a dark eyebrow at her. "And what was that for, lady?"

Leah lay her head against his shoulder. "Just making sure that you're real, and that this is not a dream."

"You have a sweet voice, my Leah. I'm glad you can talk now."

Laughter bubbled through her. "I'm glad too – that was the worst part of the mermaid thing. Not being able to tell you anything that was going on." Impulsively, she hugged his neck and giggled against his hair. She felt as giddy with excitement. "I can't believe I get to stay!"

He set her down, gently, a troubled look on his familiar, dear face. "Won't you miss your home? This 'Seattle' that she mentioned?"

Leah shook her head, slipping her hand into his and taking an experimental step forward. None of the tingling associated with every step for the past month followed her. No reminder of her mermaid tail. It was as if it had never happened. "Seattle holds nothing for me, anymore," she said happily. "My world is here with you."

"We'll get married within a fortnight," he stated flatly, squeezing her hand tight. "The king will insist on being there, or I'd make it sooner. He told me he wanted to meet the woman that had saved my fortune from Baron Rutledge." A gentle smile touched his lips. "I wasn't sure he would get the chance."

Nervous excitement shot through her. "I wasn't either, but I'm glad." A dark thought occurred to her and she frowned, her spirits drooping a little. "Will it matter very much that I'm not noble?"

"I'm the bastard son of an unimportant noble, so no, it does not matter."

She brightened at that. "All right, then." Feeling shy, Leah smiled up at him. "I'll become your wife."

He grabbed her by the waist and lifted her, twirling her around him as he spun, laughing. "Leah of the kingdom of Seattle has agreed to become my wife." He set her down and gave her a perplexed look. "Where is this 'Seattle'? Normandy?"

That would be a harder explanation. "It's in America. It's a long, long story, and I'm not sure if you'll believe me."

"Is it more ridiculous than a woman cursed to have a fish-tail?"

"Only slightly." Leah gave him a lopsided smile. "Will that change anything?"

He shook his head, pulling her close for a long kiss. "Nothing could change my love for you, my Leah. Even if you told me that you were from the Heavens themselves."

"Close," Leah whispered against his mouth. "Very, very close."

From the Author

Thank you for reading this book! Seriously – thank you. Somewhere out there, a unicorn just farted a rainbow out of sheer happiness. And your hair sure is pretty today! Have you lost weight? No? Well, keep doing what you're doing, because you look fabulous.

Anyhow…

If you are the type that likes to review what you've read, I'd love for you to leave me a review – let me know what you thought. Feedback is super important to people like me that juggle three or more series at once. We love feedback like chocolate loves peanut butter. And the more feedback I get, the more it tells me what I need to work on next. So if you want more Time Travel books, let me know!

About the Author

Jessica Clare is a New York Times and USA Today Bestselling author who writes under three different names. As Jill Myles, she writes a little bit of everything, from sexy, comedic urban fantasy to zombie fairy tales. As Jessica Clare, she writes erotic contemporary romance.

She also has a third pen name (because why stop at two?). As Jessica Sims, she writes fun, sexy shifter paranormals. She lives in Texas with her husband, cats, and too many dust-bunnies. Jill spends her time writing, reading, writing, playing video games, and doing even more writing.

JILL MYLES

CPSIA information can be obtained at www.ICGtesting.com
Printed in the USA
LVOW06s2107260815

451631LV00003B/264/P